SAFE WHERE THE NORTH WIND BLOWS

Ann M. Pratley

Another blow to the side of the head was what it took to convince Monica Tennyson that it must be time - it must be *past* time, in fact, that her husband, Ricky, had reached the threshold of what Monica could take in terms of his abuse.

"I said pick that mop up and CLEAN IT UP!" she heard her deadbeat husband yell at her one more time, as if she was hard of hearing. In truth, it was surprising she wasn't, given how much of his yelling she'd endured since their daughter, Patricia, had been born. Every time it happened, Monica couldn't understand herself at all. She kept staying with the asshole. Why? What was it about him that kept her by his side, putting up with all that he'd already put her through, and *continued* to put her through, day after day after day?

For that split moment, she considered picking up that mop alright, but not to clean up the mess Ricky had made when he'd thrown a tantrum about the meal Monica had prepared. No, it would have been far more satisfying to pick up that mop and shove that handle right up…

She'd only just thought she was already at the end of her tether with what she was willing to endure to keep her child safe, before she was proved wrong. Without moving away, she took the next blow that came. She then started to perform the task he'd told her to, not because she cared about being beaten herself, but because she knew she needed to remain alive in order to get her daughter out of that house and to anywhere safe.

For that whole night she lay awake, thinking. As always, she endured Ricky having his way with her. The romantic side of that had ended long ago. Now it was more like a punishment that, again, she would endure until she didn't have to any more.

She'd had plenty of nights like the one she was currently living – nights where she planned to get away in the morning. Every time she had a night like that, she got up the following morning, prepared to leave, and then just about walked out the door. Then, when it was finally time to go … she didn't. Why? That was the question she'd never been able to successfully answer. In truth, she had no idea why she'd never actually turned her back on him and walked out that door. Logically, it made absolutely no sense to stay, but she always had.

She knew things had to change. They had to. If for nothing else and no other reason, her daughter was worth staying alive for.

Yes, it was true she'd been planning an escape for a very long time. It was also true that whenever she'd thought it was time to put an escape plan into action, and that she could do it, something in the back of her mind had stopped her. Still the same questions came. Why did she stay? Was it out of fear? Was it out of some twisted kind of devotion to the man she honestly thought she'd once loved, even though she could hardly summon any memory of that now? None of it made any logical sense, even to her, and yet day after day everything was always the same and nothing ever changed.

But now something finally felt like it had.

When the long night had passed, and Ricky finally left their home to go to wherever he went during the daytime hours, Monica scooped up her daughter and ran. She didn't stop to pack. She didn't stop to get cash from an ATM. She didn't stop for anything. She just needed to get to that large brick building two blocks from home.

That was all she had to do …

Run …

CHAPTER 2

As she sat in her local police precinct, Monica held her three year old daughter, Patricia, close to her chest. Although logic told her she was in a safe place and Ricky couldn't get to her where she was, she naturally looked around her, again and again, as if an animal that knew a predator was out there somewhere, even if it couldn't be seen. The fear inside of her was immense, but it was a fear that she knew she was better to feel in that building, than the fear she constantly felt when she was in the place she used to enjoy calling home.

The previous two days had been almost unbearable, having to pretend to want to stay with her husband, while knowing the right thing to do to ensure the safety of herself and her daughter was to finally take the plunge and do anything to get far, far away. That was something she was still determined to do, but not before she'd filed a report against her husband, ensuring it was known and recorded what he'd done and how he'd treated her, not just on that night before, but for years.

Despite her nervousness and apprehension over what she'd decided to do, Monica forced herself to hold her head high as she went through an interview process like she'd never experienced before.

"And you say he beat you?" the law enforcement officer asked her.

"Not every day but yes, often," Monica replied, trying to force the memories away while knowing she had to confront them to complete the process. "I know it probably doesn't seem that important but…" she started to say, as if it really wasn't important that she'd been hit over and over, sometimes truly savagely.

"We do have some concerns about your husband, Mrs Tennyson," another officer said, surprising her. "In fact, he's been on our radar for quite some time."

"He ... he's been ... I'm sorry, I'm not sure what you're saying," said Monica. "I haven't been in here to talk about him before. This is the first time I've reported him..."

"Yes, of course, but are you aware of ... other aspects of his life, Mrs Tennyson?" she heard, the questions beginning to take an odd turn of direction.

Before answering, Monica took her time to try and process what she'd just been asked. Had she known anything about 'other aspects of his life'? As hard as she tried to consider if she had, she could only reply in full honesty.

"No," she said. "He ... he ... he isn't the person I thought I was marrying, but ... but he goes to work each morning and he comes home each evening," Monica said. "I'm sorry but what ... what are you asking, exactly?"

As Monica watched, she saw the investigators glance at each other before both refocused on her.

"It is timely that you've come to see us today," one officer said. "We believe that, given what you've told us, it would be best for you to leave..."

"I know that if I do, and he finds me, he could kill me," Monica said, not entirely sure if the words she'd used had been spoken flippantly, or spoken with an underlying suspicion of truth and expectation.

"As I said, we think it would be best for you and your daughter to leave, without any delay," she heard. "We have everything in place to be able to help you."

"You have ... everything in place?" Monica asked, only growing more confused by the minute. "To help me? But I only walked in here an hour ago..."

Once again, she watched the officers share a look that she didn't know the meaning of. She'd thought it bad enough what had been going on behind closed doors with her husband. Was there even worse to learn about him? Had he fooled her throughout *all* of the years they'd been together?

"We'd like to get you into witness protection … immediately," one of the officers said, his facial expression telling her there was no possible way they were joking. "Two of our officers can take both of you right now…"

"Take us? Where?" Monica asked. She'd already decided that was the day she would try and get away, but hearing someone else tell her everything was in place to help them do so seemed a bit too coincidental, no matter how tempting it sounded. "Sorry but I don't understand any of this. Where do you want to take us? Witness protection? For witnessing him hitting me? People don't get put into witness protection for that … do they? I don't know what you're saying, and I don't know what to do! We can't go home…"

"No, you shouldn't," the investigator told her. "Mrs Tennyson, we have everything in place to help you and your daughter start over."

"A new life," the other officer said. "In a new location far away from here – somewhere your husband won't find you."

Listening to what she was being told, Monica was stunned at how the conversation had turned. She'd married a man she'd truly believed was a good man, and he had seemed to be until Patricia had come along. Since then, everything had gone downhill in so many ways.

The more the investigators spoke, with their implication that they knew more about her husband than she did, the more understanding she gained about how little she might know her husband after all. She didn't want to know more than she needed to but if the local police were already set up to help her and Patricia leave town and start a new life, that had to mean they knew something far more serious about Ricky than she did -

something that they were building a case against him with, if they thought she should be in witness protection.

Realizing the degree of danger could be far greater than even she could have guessed after his treatment of her already, was there any reason she should argue and not do whatever they suggested?

Hugging Patricia closer to her chest, she closed her eyes and breathed in the scent of her daughter. There were many aspects of life that she'd always considered important, but Patricia was by far the most important of all. No matter how much Monica could put up with, she wouldn't expose her daughter to anything more that represented the worst aspects of humankind.

"Okay," she said after running all possibilities through her mind. She didn't know what they were watching Ricky for, and nobody seemed forthcoming in telling her why it might be important she was whisked away and put somewhere safe. She supposed that when the time came, they would have to tell her. Could she live with the unknowing until then? After contemplation, she knew the answer was yes. Yes she could.

"Okay?" one investigator asked. "Okay, you are on board with us helping you and your daughter to get away and start a new life?"

"Yes," Monica replied.

"And you understand this will happen immediately?" the investigator continued. "We won't risk letting you go home, Mrs Tennyson. To go now means that we go *now*."

"Yes ... but ... how does it work exactly?" Monica asked as a sliver of doubt began to flow over her again. "I have nothing. I mean, do I go to a bank and try to withdraw cash before we go? How do I get money for us to live off? Do I get a job? I have nothing. What ... how ...?

"We understand this is a lot to think about but you

don't need to worry about anything like that right now," she heard. "We have everything in place for you – a new identity, including IDs, and a place for you and your daughter to live. We'll also help you financially to begin with so there's no digital trace of you for your husband to find."

"Is ... is it far away?" she asked, feeling like she'd just jumped into a tornado. This was one day out of many that she'd considered running away from Ricky, and this was also the day that the police were ready to help her escape? The odds of that seemed astronomically impossible. But here they were, telling her they could help her and Patricia to start a new life in a safe place, away from her abuser. 'Witness protection', they'd said. That meant ... yes, there had to be a case being built against Ricky. What was it for, and when was she going to learn any details about it? He'd proven he was a monster who could disguise himself as a gentleman, but not for too long before cracks began to appear in the polite mask he could wear. Had he done even worse to other people than what he'd done to her?

"Alaska – a small town called Skagway," she heard the investigator reply over the top of the thoughts and questions plaguing her mind.

"Right," said Monica, suddenly remembering back to a previous time – a happier time. "Yes, I've been there – stopped there for a few hours on a cruise years ago."

"We need to know what your answer is, Mrs Tennyson," the investigator said. "Say yes and we can help you walk out of this precinct, and get you and your daughter on your way to safety."

It was a big thing to think about but Monica hesitated no more. She'd given enough time to someone who can't have loved her, no matter how much he'd said he did. No, people who loved one another didn't treat each other like that. And if she stayed and there was something far worse the police were investigating regarding Ricky, where was it going to end for her? Death? No, for Patricia's sake, Monica knew she couldn't let that happen.

"Yes," she said, pushing the last of her doubt and uncertainty aside. "Yes!"

"As we said, you'll have a new identity, and it starts today," one investigator said as he pushed an envelope across the table. "Stacy McNab."

"Stacy," Monica repeated as she contemplated no longer being the person she'd been her entire life. "Stacy McNab. I always liked the name Stacy. And Patricia?"

"When it comes to children, we think it could be confusing for her if you start to use an entirely different name…."

"Patti," Monica – now Stacy – said when she pulled another piece of paper from the envelope. "Patti McNab. I can do that."

Within the hour, she and Patricia were at the local airport, flanked by two strict-looking law enforcement officers in plain clothing. It wasn't a quick trip to the small town she'd been told was going to be her new home, but even getting to the boarding gate made Monica – Stacy – feel like infinite possibilities lay ahead for her and her daughter.

Every step of the way, she kept looking around and behind her, just in case, but Ricky wasn't there. He wasn't there the first time she looked, or the second, or the third. When she was finally on board the first plane, she kept watching the passengers boarding, still with the expectation that he could walk in at any moment. To her growing relief, he didn't.

Finally she felt the exhilaration of that first plane taking off. She was on board with her daughter, and her husband wasn't. Close by were two men who were going to escort her all the way. Both were clean cut, smelling heavenly and wearing classy suits, looking like regular businessmen. If Ricky had gotten to her somehow, would they really have had the skills to protect her? Stacy allowed herself only a moment of contemplating that scenario before she pushed the question from her mind. He wasn't on the plane, so the question didn't need to be asked.

"Patti cakes, Patti cakes," she started to quietly say as she remembered a children's rhyme her mother had told her when she'd been a child. When she saw her daughter look up at her, deliver an amazing grin and then repeat the words, Stacy laughed. Who knew what lay ahead for both of them. The unknowing was both scary and invigorating.

Relaxing back in the seat, for a moment she felt completely alone. How long would she feel like that? Beside her was her daughter, who always made her happy. In seats very close to where she and Patti sat, she knew the sharp looking escorts were also there, keeping an eye on her with the promise of keeping her safe all the way to where her new life would begin.

Turning to look at them, she caught the eye of one of the men – Chad Andrews, he'd said his name was, although whether that was his real name, she couldn't have any idea. Seeing him give her a reassuring smile, she guessed she should have been happy. He appeared to be a completely different kind of man to the one she'd invested too much time with, and probably would have made some women blush on receipt of that smile. Inside, Stacy knew she would never have an interest in romance again in her life. No, it was far too easy to be fooled into a dreamy falsehood of romance, only to then wake up in a complete nightmare. Although she smiled back at her well-groomed and perfectly mannered escort, all she felt inside was numb, and that was how she'd felt for a very long time.

CHAPTER 3

With each flight they caught on their way to a new life, Stacy felt herself relaxing a little bit more, and then a little bit more again. Next to her was her little Patricia – now Patti. Every time Stacy looked at her, she knew she'd made the right decision. She hadn't stood completely on her own two feet before, entirely responsible for everything to do with raising a child, but she was determined that she could. In truth, any life she could give Patti without having to witness what she already might have, had to be a better life than they'd been living. It had to be!

She didn't consider herself strong, like she knew other women were, but she could do it. She could begin to live a new life – a safe life – and raise Patti as she always should have been raised, in a home free of violent actions and violent speech. Even if they ended up being poor financially, at least she knew it cost nothing to give her daughter time, attention and love.

"Not long now," she heard her escort, Chad, say from his final seat across the aisle from her. "This is a nice little town. Have you been here before?"

In reply, Stacy forced herself to smile at him again. In truth she was nervous about what lay ahead, but for the entire trip the two officers had discretely directed her in where to go and what to do. The one who'd spoken to her certainly might not have been regarded as good looking by some, but Stacy couldn't deny she felt a strong pull toward him, and very safe in his presence. Even without him saying much at all, there was something very powerful emanating from him. Having him close by was almost like that feeling Stacy could remember getting when she was a much younger woman, when a man would embrace her. It had all seemed so easy back then, with the future looking so positive. How had everything turned out so differently to how she'd imagined it would?

"Yes, but only briefly," she replied before diverting her attention back to her daughter once again. In that fleeting moment she wondered if she might ever have a loving relationship in her life. That thought was cut short as reality set in again. She'd only just gotten away from a relationship, and it hadn't been any kind of relationship that any woman should be in. She certainly would *not* be in any hurry to meet someone new, no matter how things went in her new life. Her heart had been open to love once upon a time. Now it was tightly closed.

As the small plane approached Skagway at the end of the long three-flight journey, Stacy glanced out the window. Seeing the light scattering of snow and greenery of trees covering the hillsides; the water that large and small vessels were dotted over; and the small township with its main street that looked like it had been made for a western movie set, Stacy felt her emotions move from one extreme to another.

Was it a happy day? A sad day? A scary day? For a moment she wasn't sure which emotion was the right one to focus on. When she again glanced at the small person in the next seat, looking up at her with only happiness on her face, that was the emotion Stacy knew she had to try and portray, even if she only felt it for seconds at a time.

After disembarking, Stacy walked through the tiny terminal building, following the two officers who had been on the plane with her. She'd been instructed to not talk to them, as if she didn't know who they were, but she'd also been instructed to follow them and get into a waiting car with them after walking out. The confusion about everything was enough to cause minor moments of panic. To get through those moments, she had to keep looking at her daughter. Seeing that funny smile that never housed any worry or sadness was always enough to make Stacy the happiest mom in the world.

Once inside the waiting vehicle, she relaxed back in the back seat, along with Patti. Sitting behind the officer who'd introduced himself as Chad, Stacy found herself distracted for a moment by the immaculate, clean cut hairstyle he had, and the strong scent of men's aftershave that she'd always loved. As she caught herself focusing on such a thing, she let herself smile as she diverted her attention to the vista outside of the car. Far more important things lay ahead for her to focus on than how good a man smelt.

"Come with us," she heard him say when the car stopped only a short distance away.

Inside the local sheriff's station, her escorts finally left her side as Stacy was introduced to the town's sheriff, Sheriff Reed. Although he was welcoming, it seemed like hours that she sat and listened to details about how she would live her new life, and the do's and don'ts of being in witness protection. It was a lot to take in, but Stacy was resolved to follow all instructions given to keep her and Patti safe.

"My deputy, here, will escort you to your new home, Stacy," she heard the sheriff finally say as a young woman officer walked into the room. It wasn't the first time someone had addressed Stacy, using her new name, but each time someone did, it still surprised her. That was something she knew she was going to have to work hard at – remembering who she was now – as she worked equally hard at trying to forget who she'd once been.

"Thank you," Stacy said to the sheriff before beginning to follow the young woman out of the station.

As they were walking out, Stacy smelt the familiar scent. Looking up, she again saw the friendlier one of the two officers who'd escorted her and Patti to Skagway. No words were exchanged but as they approached one another in the corridor, she indulged in taking a moment to breathe in that same scent of male cologne. When she exhaled with a feeling of calm flowing over her, she realized Chad was subtly smiling at her, almost as if he'd caught her in her moment of wanting to smell him. It was the first time in a very long time that Stacy felt herself blush.

"My car's just out here," she heard the deputy say as they approached the door.

Behind her, Stacy knew Chad Andrews was walking toward the sheriff's office. She dared not turn to look at him again, even though she surprisingly felt drawn to.

"I'm sorry – what should I call you?" she asked the deputy, wanting to distract herself and realizing nobody had mentioned the young woman's name.

"Everyone calls me by my last name here," the deputy said, grinning as she helped Stacy settle Patti into a car seat that had already been installed into the police car. "Smithy, you can call me."

"Smithy," said Stacy, returning the smile. "Well, thank you Smithy for helping us."

"Your new place is just here," the deputy said when the car pulled into a small driveway a short time later. "It's not flash but it's ..."

"Cute," Stacy said as she glanced over the tiny home in front of her. "And cute is more than adequate for us. All I want, Smithy, is some time to be in peace."

"Well, you've come to the right place for that," said Smithy as they all climbed out of the vehicle. "Just look around and breathe in the fresh air. Man, I love this town!"

Seeing the look of contentment on the deputy's face, Stacy smiled. In recent times, it had felt as though she hadn't had much to smile about at all. Following the deputy's suggestion and looking around, taking in the vista of the trees on the surrounding hills and the water in the distance, she realized how little time she'd ever spent in nature. She'd always been a city girl. That was about to change.

CHAPTER 4

"No, no, NO!" Stacy heard her own voice say as she woke from her deep sleep on that first night. Turning to pick up the simple no-bells-and-whistles phone she'd been issued, she saw 3:04am on the screen. Whatever she'd just been having a nightmare about, that was all it had been – just a bad dream.

As her consciousness sharpened, she turned onto her back and just listened. Only the night before, she'd been in her marital bed, listening to Ricky snore as she had remained as still as she could, afraid to move in case she woke him up. In recent times, that had been just one scenario that would anger him and send him into a rage – if he woke up and she was beside him. If that happened, it was always her fault that he'd woken too soon.

Lying alone, she felt relief from there being no body close to her. There was no snoring and there wasn't even the sound of breathing. To her surprise, there was also an odd loneliness that came from that, even though she knew she'd made the right choice in leaving.

What would he have thought when he'd returned home later that day and found her and Patti gone? Would he have been worried about where they were, concerned that something might have happened to them? Or would he have been enraged that she wasn't there, cooking his meal at the exact time he wanted it to be ready?

Delving deeper into her thoughts about how he might have reacted, Stacy began to truly wonder what he might have done. Anyone else might have called law enforcement if their partner and child were missing, but the police had obviously been watching Ricky for quite some time, and appeared to know far more about him than Stacy did. Would he have risked going near the police station to report her and Patti missing, if it meant interacting with the police at all?

After some time of consideration about what he might or might not have done, Stacy forced herself to smile. In the darkness, she lay in a bed alone, in a room alone, and there was no longer any threat from the man she'd loved and married. Although she knew she should now embrace the happier situation she was in, she did suddenly feel that vibe of loneliness flow over her again. It was ridiculous that it should exist, given what he'd put her through, but it was what it was.

With her mind not rested enough to get back to sleep quite yet, she carefully pulled back the covers and stood. Her little Patti was in the next room. Were there creaks on the floorboards of their new home that might wake her if Stacy moved in the night? Everything was unknown about the new life they were embarking upon - even the location of floorboard creaks.

Despite the uncertainty about whether she might somehow wake her daughter or not, Stacy tiptoed into the next room. Before her, Patti lay sleeping deeply, snuggled almost completely under the covers, just as if she wasn't in a foreign bed at all. The sight made Stacy smile. She was safe, and her daughter was safe. How it had all fallen into place so easily, she still couldn't fathom. She was just thankful it had. Whatever fate had in store for her and Patti, it was reassuring that Stacy could rest for the moment, at least a little, knowing that whatever Patti had witnessed so far in her short lifetime, she would now not see anything more of again.

With the unexpected loneliness slipping away on seeing her daughter at peace, Stacy finally retraced her steps, sunk back into her new bed, gave consideration one more time to her now being 'Stacy McNab', and was soon fast asleep again.

CHAPTER 5

"You seem determined," Chad Andrews heard a deep voice say from the doorway of the small office he'd been assigned. Looking up, he saw Sheriff Reed looking at him with what looked like an expression of amusement. "Do you really think you'll uncover what happened to that girl, and who did it?"

As Chad glanced over the five large boxes of files in front of him, he sighed. He loved working on cold cases, but he equally knew it was a job that took much patience, determination, and the ability to consider facts that were recorded long ago, alongside any new facts that were yet to be discovered. Sometimes time hindered an investigation. Sometimes it helped. There were never any guarantees of success, but it was always worth it to complete a brand new search for the unknown answers.

"Let's hope so! Either way, I have to try," Chad replied. "Missy Jameson may be gone, but her family still deserves to know what happened to her."

"It's been two years," the sheriff said, doubt heavy in his voice.

"I know, but I'm here and this is what I do, so you may as well use me while you can," said Chad, grinning. In truth, he still found himself thinking about the mother and daughter he'd helped move to Skagway the day before. There had been nothing outstanding about the woman, and they'd hardly spoken at all, but he couldn't deny that she had entered his mind during the night.

"True," said the sheriff, breaking into Chad's thoughts. "They say you're a cold case expert, so I'm definitely going to use you for that while you're here!"

Before Chad could reply, he saw the sheriff walk off, shaking his head and chuckling as if he'd just heard or said a great joke. It certainly wasn't the strangest thing Chad had seen during his long career in law enforcement, but it was still more than a little odd.

Selecting the first box to work through, he carefully piled the others into a corner of the room and returned to his desk. When Missy Jameson had disappeared, she'd only been sixteen. Her disappearance had rocked the small town of Skagway, as well as people from neighboring areas. Nothing like that had happened for as long as anyone could remember, and all of the people who'd been interviewed at the time had only said good things about the young woman. She'd never been in any trouble with the law, and she'd never even gotten into any trouble at her school. As far as Chad could tell from what he'd learned already, she'd just been a quiet girl who'd lived a quiet life in a quiet town. Friendly but not too friendly. Serious but not too serious. What, then, could have happened to her?

It was often the way with missing persons investigations, he knew. The victim was almost always someone who was loved by all. Sometimes, as investigations progressed, it was revealed that someone wasn't loved by *all* after all, and some people weren't as sad over a person going missing as they'd initially indicated to police. Although that was certainly sometimes the truth, Chad's gut told him it might not be the case with Missy. When she'd disappeared, she had hardly started to live at all. At that age, and in that location, how much trouble could she have possibly gotten herself into anyway?

Delving into the first few files of details about Missy's life, Chad settled deeper into the chair that would be his own for as long as it took to resolve the case. He'd been in law enforcement for a great number of years but when he'd been given a first chance to work on a cold case, he'd found himself hooked by the challenge of it. There was always sadness in anyone being hurt or killed, especially young people, but Chad found another level of sadness in cases where families had received no answers about what had happened to their loved ones. It was a scenario he continuously found himself wanting to work hard in so he could hopefully provide at least a little closure to people still suffering.

There was much to read about Missy Jameson on that first day, even though there was little to suggest anything other than her having been a good student, a good friend, and a good daughter. One thing Chad had learned from his career to date was that sometimes there was something lurking under the surface of any human, and sometimes that was what was needed to be found in order to find the person themselves.

At the end of some intense reading, assessing, and note taking to build a list of people to speak to the following day, his mind again surprisingly returned to the woman and child he'd escorted to Skagway the day before. She'd already invaded his thoughts the night before, and he wasn't sure he liked her doing it again. Not that it was her doing, of course, but still … what was it about her that made his mind want to keep drifting back to her?

It was true there was something about her that seemed familiar to Chad, but he was sure he'd never met her. Was it just that she was an attractive woman and she'd secured his attention because of her looks? No, he'd never been a man who was attracted to women because of how they looked. The few he'd been involved with in his lifetime had all become partners following a long period of friendship. That had always been far more important to Chad than the outer appearance of anyone – the ability to be a great friend, and the ability to show strength when needed, but also vulnerability.

Perhaps that was what made him think of the woman and her child. Although he'd been one of the officers to escort her to Skagway, he hadn't been told anything about her except that the two of them were being relocated and needed escorts. Chad had been in law enforcement long enough to believe that would mean they were in some form of witness protection, but he'd also been in law enforcement long enough to know that only a select few ever knew the details about those cases. If the woman and her daughter were in that predicament, Chad had only been their travel escort, and not anyone who needed to know what the story was behind their relocation.

Scoffing at himself for yet again being distracted, he looked up at the time and was surprised to see it was already close to 6pm. His mind could keep going for hours yet but his body was telling him it was clearly time to knock off, go and enjoy a good meal, and then relax for the evening to let his mind process all that he'd read that day. Sometimes it was pushing the brain harder that worked in a cold case. More often than not, success came from making sure to let the brain be settled and clear, and to do its natural job of assessment and calculation.

With that thought, Chad Andrews placed the files he'd read into the desk drawer, grabbed his jacket, and set off for the night.

CHAPTER 6

"Good morning!" Stacy heard her elderly neighbor call out to her from their front yard. After an initial few days of staying indoors out of fear she might be seen or recognized, she'd finally ventured out with Patti on each of the previous two days. Even though she'd been told there was no way Ricky could find them, it still seemed more than a little nerve-wracking being out and about in public, but she forced herself to try and seem normal. That was the only way she would be able to raise Patti with normality – to act like this was not only their life now, but had always been.

"Good morning!" Stacy called back as she waved. Inside she wondered if she would ever feel like she could trust anyone again, but she tried as hard as she could to not show that uncertainty.

"It's a beautiful day," her neighbor said as she moved closer. "I know you're new to the area but if you haven't already been up to the waterfall, I highly recommend a visit up that way with the weather now fining up."

"A waterfall?" Stacy asked. She'd never been into nature at all in her lifetime, but there was certainly something appealing about the sound and sight of such a thing.

"Yes, if you walk up this way, you'll see signs pointing the way to the old cemetery," said the neighbor. "That in itself is quite something to see. I used to love walking up there and reading the old gravestones. This town has such a history you know!"

Seeing the woman smile one more time and then turn away to return to her garden chores, Stacy felt inquisitive. Did she feel strong enough to walk to a remote part of town that she hadn't seen before? The waterfall sounded tempting. Being somewhere remote and away from the small but general population of the township didn't.

"Have a good day," she called out to the woman before she took Patti's hand in hers and began to walk what had become a normal route for them. It was only around a few square blocks, but she couldn't deny it felt good to be out in the crisp fresh air and getting some exercise. Both were things they'd missed experiencing in recent times.

As they walked past what looked to be a school, Stacy stopped and glanced through the fence at the children playing in the grounds. Patti wasn't old enough to be going to school yet but, when she was, would she be going to school in this town? Or could something unhappy happen that would have them long gone from their peaceful new home by then? Stacy still didn't know what was going to be expected of her from law enforcement in exchange for her and Patti being relocated. In part, she hoped she would find out soon so it could then be over with. At the same time, she also found herself hoping it might take years before she'd be required to do whatever it was that she was going to have to do – years of silence and peace hopefully.

"Stacy," she heard a friendly voice call out. Turning, she saw the same deputy she'd met on her first night in Skagway.

"Smithy!" Stacy said, grinning. They'd run into each other a couple of times since her arrival in the small township, and each time the deputy had greeted her as if she'd known her for years. It was a relatively new experience for Stacy, but it was also nice.

"Thinking of signing this little one up?" Smithy asked as she smiled at Patti.

"Oh, no, she's too young yet," said Stacy.

"Yeah, for the main school, I guess, but has anyone

talked to you about the preschool?"

"Preschool? No," Stacy replied. "There's one here?"

"Yeah, it's part of this, and on these grounds, but the younger kids have their own classroom and play area that's fenced off so they don't interact with these older kids," said Smithy. "Two of my sister's kids are here at the school, and her youngest is in the preschool. If you wanna take a look, I can escort you in there now…"

"Oh, I'm not sure," Stacy said, feeling an almost overwhelming sense of unease flow over her.

For a long moment, she saw the deputy look at her as if studying her and understanding completely that Stacy had some fears that weren't anywhere close to being overcome.

"Yeah, of course. No problem at all," said Smithy. "But you have my number. Just let me know if you wanna go and have a look and I'll happily come in and introduce you to the teacher in there."

"Thank you," said Stacy, relieved that she wouldn't have to go into any discussion about her doubts. "But, Smithy, the lady who lives next to us just told me about a … waterfall … and a … cemetery? Do you know where she might have meant?"

"Yes!" Smithy replied, grinning. "I haven't been up there for years, to be honest, but when I was a teenager I loved hanging out there. Yeah, it's a nice spot. Do you wanna go up? I can give you guys a ride up so you know where it is at least."

"Is … is it … safe up there?" Stacy asked. "My neighbor said it was nice but it also sounded kind of remote."

"It is a bit away from the town but we've never had any serious incidents up there or anything," said Smithy. "Occasionally some teens will head up there and think it's cool to get drunk around the graveyard – you know the drill, experiment just as we all did when we were that age – but they don't tend to get into trouble, and they aren't usually there early in the day." She waited for Stacy to consider her offer. "I have a little free time now if you'd like to take a quick look. I can take you…"

"Okay," Stacy said, pushing herself to be proactive instead of afraid. "Yes, thank you, Smithy. If you're sure you have time, I would love for you to show us where it is."

"Okily dokily," Smithy said. "Let me just get the old car seat set up and we'll be on our way!"

Half an hour later, with Patti secure in her arms, Stacy walked amid graves that captured her attention, as did the sound of water falling in the distance.

"This is the way to the waterfall," she heard Smithy say as she pointed toward a small track. "It's safe to walk, and, if I remember correctly, it's an easy walk."

A few minutes later, before her was the first waterfall Stacy had ever seen in real life. Despite never having had any interest in being in nature, she instantly felt a level of calm she'd been seeking for a very long time.

"It's beautiful, isn't it," Smithy said, grinning. "It's been far too long since I last came up here but, honestly, this is the best spot around here for de-stressing."

"It is beautiful," Stacy agreed. "Thank you for bringing us here."

"No problem at all. I have to get back to work soon so can't stay for long but do you guys want to stay here and walk back? Or else I can give you a ride back now," Smithy said.

As much as Stacy found herself surprised by how much she felt at peace in the environment, she took a deep breath and smiled.

"We'll come back to town with you now, if that's okay," she said. "But I'll definitely return another day."

"Yes! Make sure you do!" said Smithy before turning and beginning to lead their trek back down to the car. "And think about putting this little lady in preschool too. I know everything is new for you here, and I can't imagine how hard that is, but getting to know new people will be good for you and Patti both. It's a small town, and it can be deadly quiet in winter, but there really are some wonderful characters living here year round."

"I'll keep that in mind," Stacy replied with as much enthusiasm as she could muster. Although she'd been in Skagway long enough to start feeling a little at ease, fear and uncertainly still seemed never too far away.

CHAPTER 7

While Chad Andrews worked his way through the files of the cold case disappearance of Missy Jameson, he broke up his days by going out and interviewing everyone in the Skagway region who had given a statement previously. He hoped someone might remember something they'd overlooked mentioning at the time of the young girl's disappearance.

As the days passed and he moved through the list, he felt his belief in being able to solve the case slowly deplete. It was always the way, he knew, with moments on every case where he was left wondering if the answers would ever be found. He also knew that more often than not, a case was finally resolved, even years after it had begun. Not always, but certainly often.

Walking up to the fifth person he'd interviewed for the day, he saw an elderly man eagerly ripping out weeds of his front garden. When the man seemed to sense Chad approaching, and turned to face him, Chad silently took note of the look of unhappiness on the man's face.

"I've been expecting you," the man said as he slowly rose to stand.

"Mr Simpson?" Chad asked to clarify it was the man he'd hoped to find.

"Yes, but then you know that," the man said. "That's why you're here, isn't it? To see me."

"Mr Simpson, I'm Chad Andrews..." Chad started to say before the man turned and started to walk toward his front door.

"I know who you are," Mr Simpson said as he stepped over the threshold of his home. "You're looking into Missy's disappearance. Sheriff Reed already told me you'd be coming to talk to me."

Chad stood still, unsure what to think of the brash way the man was speaking to him. He was used to cold receptions whenever he embarked on a case. He'd never understood that since he was only trying to find out what happened to someone. Sometimes he'd found himself wondering if family and friends even *wanted* to know what had happened to their loved ones, their reception had been so cold.

"Come on then," the elderly man suddenly said, prompting Chad to finally move forward. "Take a seat there and I'll make the coffee."

Not daring to say that he didn't even like coffee, Chad followed the direction to sit down, and patiently began to wait. He'd read Mr Simpson's original statement that had been taken when Missy had first gone missing. There had been little to it, but Chad still felt he had to follow it up.

"I don't think there's anything new I can tell you," Mr Simpson finally said when he placed two cups on the table and sat down, facing Chad. "What I said back then is all that I know for sure, although…"

"Yes?" Chad prompted, curious about what the elderly man could be about to say.

"Look, the thing is that I knew little Missy, and she was a good girl," said Mr Simpson. "Some people reckoned she ran away but I never thought that was likely."

"Why do you think that?" Chad asked.

"Because she was a good girl!" Mr Simpson replied. "I spent years working at the local high school, and I think I have a good radar when it comes to good kids and not-so-good kids. Missy was a good one."

"Right," said Chad. "You said you know what you said back when it happened, *although*. Since that time, have you remembered something else about when she disappeared?"

"No, I don't remember anything new … hardly remember much at all these days! … but I have … at times … wondered…."

Chad sat forward, intrigued. Everyone he'd spoken to so far had stood by their original statement, with nothing new to add at all. Mr Simpson seemed about to say something new. What could that new something be?

"Any thought or opinion is appreciated, Mr Simpson," Chad said. "What is it that you seem to want to say?"

The two men sat in silence for a long while, studying each other as if trying to suss each other out. Finally Mr Simpson spoke and shared what had been on his mind for a very long time.

"Well I've always wondered … if she might be … in the cemetery," he said. "Don't ask me why I think that. It's just been a gut feeling, but I've had it for quite some time, to the point where sometimes it's felt like it's haunting me."

"But you never told the sheriff or anyone else down at the station about your thoughts?" Chad asked and saw the man slowly shake his head, his face revealing a degree of what looked like regret.

"I did tell the sheriff when I first felt that inkling, but he made it clear he had no interest in hearing people's 'feelings', and there's nothing solid behind this thought," Mr Simpson said. "Like I said, it's been a gut feeling – a strong one, admittedly, but nothing more. The last thing I'd want to do is keep pushing something like that and get the case re-opened, giving the family hope that wouldn't be based on anything real…"

Chad nodded in understanding. He knew even from his history of working on cold cases that there was every chance he would be giving a family some new hope, and only end up putting them through misery all over again if he couldn't solve the case.

"I understand," he said. "But is there really no more to your feeling about this? You didn't hear somebody say something about Missy, or about the cemetery…"

"No, like I say, it's just a feeling I had," Mr Simpson replied. "Sometimes I have those – feelings about different things – and sometimes they turn out to be true, but not always. I wish I could provide something more … concrete … but I can't, and it probably means nothing at all."

"Sure, so … you think she might be … buried … in Pioneer Cemetery?" Chad asked, having visited that location after his initial study of case notes.

"No!" Mr Simpson exclaimed. "Not *Pioneer Cemetery*!"

"Oh? Forgive me, Mr Simpson," said Chad. "I'm still getting to know my way around Skagway. Are you saying … is there *another* cemetery here?"

"Yes! Like I told the sheriff back then, the gut feeling I have always had is that she might be in the *Gold Rush* Cemetery!"

"I see," Chad said as he hurriedly began taking notes. He was still working through all of the boxes of notes associated with Missy's disappearance, but so far hadn't heard anything about the small town having a second cemetery, and he'd also never read any notes about the man's gut feeling, but that wasn't so surprising since it was only that – a feeling. "It's … wow, I would never have guessed that a town of this size…"

"It's from the gold rush days, just like the name implies," Mr Simpson said. "Hasn't been used for well over a hundred years, I don't think, but as far as old, unused cemeteries go, it's pretty popular as a place for young folk to hang out – and those horrible tourists that come in on those big ugly ships every year."

"Right, and that is the cemetery you … feel … Missy might be in? Gold Rush Cemetery?" Chad asked and saw the elderly man nod as his face showed a clear indication of annoyance at the questions. "Buried? In a grave, do you mean?"

"Well, that question I can't rightly answer," Mr Simpson replied. "All I know is … what I feel … and what I feel is that she's there."

Chad waited patiently in the hope that he might be able to glean more information from the elderly man facing him. When it appeared Mr Simpson had said all that he wanted to say, Chad thanked him and said his farewell. It was hardly anything to investigate, but the fact was that Missy Jameson was somewhere, and an old cemetery was as good a place to look as anywhere else. It wouldn't be a search he could do himself, but he figured there could be no harm in going to have a look at the place.

Following an old paper map he'd picked up, he slowly made his way through the small, sleepy town and up toward the old cemetery. Seeing the buildings of the township left behind, he remained aware of the surroundings facing him. If Missy had gone up toward that cemetery, she would have certainly been in a more remote area, and less likely to be seen if something had happened to her there.

As Chad pulled into what seemed to be a small carpark, he sat still for a long while, observing what appeared to be a small tour bus of people getting out and following the sign that clearly directed the way to the cemetery. Buses of tourists went there? What kind of cemetery could it be anyway? What kind of tour *ever* went to a cemetery? And if tours did go there, did that open up the possibility that Missy could have run into a complete stranger there – a stranger who ended up hurting her and playing a role in her disappearance?

For a long while, he sat still, wondering how long the tour bus would be there. When it didn't look like they were going to be leaving anytime soon, he prompted himself to get out and start walking in that direction. Yes, there might be a small crowd of people there, but there might also be a tour guide who could enlighten Chad to what the attraction of the cemetery actually was for people coming to visit the town.

Embarking on a small trek into the woody area, Chad briefly questioned what he was doing. There had been no depth to what Mr Simpson had said, and there was nothing else among case notes or witness statements to point towards her ever going to where he currently was. Despite his uncertainty, he kept moving forward until he could see the small group.

For several minutes he stood near the back of the crowd and listened. The tour guide was certainly full of enthusiasm for the topic he was speaking about, but Chad resolved to take note of anything he might be saying. If nothing else, perhaps if the tour guide took tours there often, and had been doing so for a long time, maybe he would have noticed if there had been any disturbance in or around the graves in recent years.

As he continued to listen to the tour guide, hoping to learn about the area and figure out why it might have been an area of interest to the elderly man he'd just spent time with, a familiar face in the distance captured his attention. As hard as he tried to maintain his focus on the tour guide's voice, Chad's head kept turning to look at the young woman he'd escorted to Skagway. She didn't appear to be a part of the tour, currently walking away from the cemetery area and further into the bush, and she was with nobody – not even her daughter.

After several minutes of working to push his interest in her aside, Chad finally broke away from the enthusiastic tales of the tour guide and began to walk in the direction he'd seen Stacy go. Through the bush he walked until finally he emerged from the somber shade of it and stood before a tall waterfall.

"Whoa," he said out loud when he absorbed the sight before him.

"I had the same reaction when I first saw it," he heard Stacy call out to him, prompting him to turn toward the sound of her voice. When he saw her, she was sitting on a large rock to the side of the water flow down the hill. For a moment, his mind tried to convince him he was looking at a mermaid. That thought he pushed away as he smiled. Working full time in the role that he did, he was serious much of the time, but that passing thought definitely deserved a smile for its silliness.

"Hey," he called back, remaining where he was at a distance from her.

"I've only just found this place but it does feel like heaven to me," Stacy continued.

Since marrying Ricky, she'd often felt like she'd lost the simple ability to converse with other people, having become as isolated as she had over their time together. It was something that had been on her mind since she and Patti had arrived in Skagway.

So many things about her had changed during the course of her marriage - so many things that she wanted to turn back time on and reverse. She would never be the same person she'd been when she'd wed, but she could certainly be closer to that than she was the day she was swept away by law enforcement to set up the new life she was currently living. "What brings you up here on this fine day? Chad, right?"

Before answering, Chad nodded in response to her second question while he took his time to once again silently wish he did the kind of job that he could easily share information about. It was one of the reasons he hadn't delved too deeply into any long term relationship since he'd embarked upon his career in law enforcement.

What kind of life could anyone have with a partner if they couldn't openly discuss what they'd seen and done each day? He knew many others in his line of work had happy, fulfilling relationships, and those relationships worked well enough, so it really wasn't a valid excuse for not getting too close to someone. Regardless, he just couldn't see how the ongoing need for secrecy could possibly work at all.

"Yep! I only just learned about the cemetery, so thought I'd come and take a look at it, and then I saw you…"

Although surprised by the last words of his comment, Stacy smiled at him as best she could. It was so hard for her to trust anyone, or fully believe that their intentions toward her could be anything good, but she knew she had to at least try and let some of her natural distrust go.

"And you thought you should follow me?" she asked. She smiled as she did, but the nervousness about the possibility, she couldn't hide.

"I did," Chad admitted, equally trying to deliver a smile even though he was nervous. "How are you finding things here? It can't be easy building a new life in a new town."

"To be honest, it feels like the first time I've been truly free in my whole life," Stacy replied as she watched him move closer to where she sat. "Not that I haven't been free, of course. I mean, I've had freedom, just…"

Where her words naturally led, she didn't want to voice. She'd spent too much time being in a situation that she hadn't been happy in. Continuing to keep it at the forefront of her mind by thinking and talking about it was the last thing she wanted to do.

"I guess if there's one place in the world to feel like you're free, this is certainly it," Chad said as he cast his eyes over the bush, the trees, the sky, and the flowing water. "Would I be intruding if I joined you for a while, or would you prefer to continue your solitude?"

"No, please come and sit," said Stacy. "Honestly, I feel blessed to be able to enjoy this, and I guess I can do it any time I like so … yeah … join me, by all means."

Despite his usual ease in talking to people, which was necessary for the job that he did, he couldn't deny there was something uneasy about the woman he sat down beside. He knew nothing about her, or about what he could even ask her. He'd been assigned to escort her to Skagway, but he'd been told nothing about her circumstance or why she and her daughter were being relocated by law enforcement. Was it due to something serious? His experience told him it must be, but it was a question he knew he couldn't ask.

"How is your daughter settling in after the move?" he asked in an attempt to find some common, easy, acceptable conversation. "Patti, is it? Is she adapting okay to this new world?"

Stacy grinned. In all the craziness that had become her life, little Patti was the one aspect that did keep her happy … and sane.

"To her, the world is just one big happy place," she said. "This is her first day spending a little time in preschool, so I'm hopeful she'll be loving being around other kids right about now. It's a new experience for her to be in a place like that, interacting with other kids … and a new experience for me, not being by her side all day long."

"She didn't get to see many children before?" Chad dared to ask.

"No," said Stacy, again annoyed that as much as she wanted the past to be in the past, it was always going to keep being asked about in one situation or another. Asked about by others, and thought about by her. "No, she's lived a fairly isolated life, but I want her to be sociable. Sitting here now, though, I can certainly appreciate solitude. It's something I haven't had in a long time, but it is soothing."

"It is," said Chad as he studied her face. He'd met a lot of people in his time – some saintly and some as bad as a human could be – but faces never ceased to surprise him. Looking at the woman in front of him, he wasn't shy in taking his time to do an assessment. Her face structure gave little away about what kind of life she'd been living, but when she turned and looked into his eyes, that was where a different story could be seen. Her eyes. Yes, there was no hiding the deep pain that resided there.

"I thought that maybe you'd only come to Skagway to escort me and Patti here, but you're still here," Stacy said, half wishing he'd stop looking at her quite so closely, but also half wishing he wouldn't stop at all. "Are you on holiday?"

"No," Chad replied, chuckling. "No, I don't do holidays too well."

"An overactive mind, huh?" asked Stacy.

"Yeah, exactly," said Chad. "When I have time to sit still and just think … well, the pictures I see in my head aren't a joy to see. One of the many great perks of my job I'm afraid."

Stacy nodded but didn't reply. She understood fully about dark images in the darkness of her mind. She was curious about the man sitting close to her, but she respected boundaries and privacy. She didn't want anyone asking too much about her, so it seemed fitting that she didn't ask too much of someone else either.

"I'll be in Skagway for a while yet," Chad said after a long period of them sitting together quietly and watching the waterfall. "Perhaps … I mean … would you like to …"

He wanted to push forward and ask her to spend more time with him, elsewhere, in a different time. As was always the case, he had no idea how long he'd be in that town, or how many hours any given day would demand of his thoughts and research. It wouldn't be fair to ask anyone to deal with what he had to deal with.

He'd given up finishing his question when he heard Stacy speak up.

"Would I like to … sit and chat to you again another time on another day?" she asked.

"Yes," Chad replied, grinning. He'd been silly to think it so serious that he might like to keep talking to her. What was wrong with that? Nothing! "Exactly. I can work crazy hours, and I don't know how long I'm going to be in town…"

"Perhaps those things don't matter when two people just want to sit together and chat sometimes," Stacy said. Deep inside of her, the interaction was making her feel a little empowered for the first time in years. It was only a glimmer of empowerment, but it felt good. "Or even just sit together in complete silence and watch water fall down a hillside."

Chad nodded and smiled before relaxing back to take some deep breaths and enjoy the beauty around him. She was right. Two people could spend time together without anything more happening – or anything romantic – and if it was enjoyable, why not?

"Oh! I need to get back and pick up Patti," Stacy eventually said as she felt her watch vibrate. Once upon a time, a very long time ago, she would have always had a phone nearby. Her marriage had stopped that, as one way Ricky controlled her isolation from everyone she'd known. Sitting next to a man while hearing the roar of the falling water, Stacy experienced a sliver of joy from knowing she'd grown to not need a device in her pocket any more. The technology the police had provided – a simple old-fashioned phone she could leave at home since there was no real reason to have it, and a watch that she could use simply for time and alarms, was more than enough.

"I can give you a lift back to town if you like," said Chad, instantly jumping to his feet.

It was natural for Stacy to reject the idea, her inbuilt fear rearing its head as she contemplated getting into a car with a stranger. Taking a moment to think through and assess that fear, she instead forced herself to smile.

"Thank you," she said. No more words were needed as the two of them embarked on the short trek through the bush, through the cemetery, and out to the sunshine of the small carpark area again.

CHAPTER 8

"Mommy!" Stacy heard Patti call out to her when she entered the preschool. It had been an almost silent journey from the waterfall to the school, but it hadn't been an uneasy silence. She'd gotten to enjoy sitting next to a man, breathing in the glorious scent of his aftershave, while quietly dealing with the raw fear that had come to be natural for her. She knew it was a fear that was unfounded. She equally knew it was something she was probably going to have to just deal with for quite a while yet.

Grinning as she lifted her daughter up into her arms, she felt a renewed level of positivity that always came from holding Patti tightly.

"How was she?" she asked when a staff member approached, wearing a beaming smile.

"It can take some kids a while to settle in, but she has handled the last few hours like a pro," the staff member replied.

"Really? Nothing for me to worry about? Are you sure?" Stacy asked, hoping she was hearing the truth.

"Nothing to worry about at all," the staff member reassured her. "For the first few minutes, she seemed a little shy but then, after one of the other little girls approached her and offered her a toy to play with, this little one just completely relaxed."

"And she's been okay with the other kids?" asked Stacy, knowing her daughter had experienced little exposure to other children in her short life to date.

"Honestly, she fitted right in. She was friendly and polite to the other kids, and when we put them all down for a small nap, she did as she was asked and went to sleep," said the staff member, grinning. "It's not so easy for all kids, but she's handled her first day here just fine.

Do you want to bring her again for another visit tomorrow?"

As hard as it was, in that moment, to imagine letting her little girl out of her sight again, especially as she held Patti tightly and realized how much she'd missed her in recent hours, Stacy nodded.

"Yes, I think she needs to be around other children," she said. "Is that okay? I don't have much money right now since we're new in town, but sometime soon I know I'm going to need to find work…"

"That's no problem at all. I understand," said the staff member. "Keep bringing her in for a few hours on each day that you feel comfortable, and when you're ready to find a job, we can chat about Patti being here for full time hours."

"Thank you for being so flexible," Stacy said as she felt an unexpected tear threaten. "I really do appreciate it."

Feeling the staff member reach out and touch her arm was almost enough to make the tears burst through in a torrent. It had been so long since she'd experienced kindness, but already a great many people were showing kindness to her and Patti in the small town.

"No problem. We hope to see you again, Miss Patti!"

Seeing her daughter smile and wave before the two of them walked out gave Stacy some relief. She wanted to protect her daughter and keep her safe from the darkness of the world, but she knew it was right to encourage Patti to be a normal kid. She'd already missed out on so much that others the same age as her would have gotten to experience.

Later that night, as she tucked her daughter into her small bed, Stacy leaned down to kiss the small forehead.

"Do you want to go back tomorrow, kiddo?" she asked the sleepy child she loved so deeply.

"Yes!" Patti said. She wasn't a kid who talked a lot, even for her age, but she did give that answer with a level of conviction that made Stacy smile.

"Okay," said Stacy. "Sleep well, Patti Cakes."

After turning one more time to glance at the small child who was already almost asleep, Stacy walked out into her tiny lounge area and relaxed down into the sofa. As was the case every night since she'd gotten away, the silence brought with it a nagging feeling that something bad was going to happen. As she did every night, she had to take some time to close her eyes and remind herself that they were now safe. They were somewhere remote, and somewhere Ricky would never find them. There was nothing to worry about.

Nothing to worry about.

Nope, nothing to worry about!

CHAPTER 9

After walking Patti to preschool the following morning, and taking some time to watch her run in her funny little way to join the other children, Stacy stepped outside and breathed in the fresh, cool air. Sure, she'd always been a city girl, but she couldn't deny there was something magical about the location she was in.

"You look content," she heard Smithy call out to her. "Need a ride?"

Stacy laughed. The town was so small that it was hard to determine why anyone would *ever* need a ride!

"Thanks, Smithy, but I'm all good," she said, approaching where the deputy had stopped the car.

"Is Patti doing okay in there?" Smithy asked, nodding toward the preschool.

"So far she's loving it, but it is only day two…"

"She's gonna be fine, Stacy," said Smithy. "The question is, what are *you* going to do during these hours when she's having lots of fun with her new friends?"

"I'm actually thinking about getting some work," Stacy said quietly. "Is that okay … with my situation? Do I need to talk to someone about it?"

"No," Smithy replied, grinning. "Sheriff Reed already said you're good to go and, actually, now that you mention it, a little bird did tell me yesterday that the small souvenir shop on 5th Ave is hoping to find someone to help out over the upcoming cruise ship season…"

"Yeah?"

"Yep," Smithy called out as she started her car again. "Head over there and have a chat with the store owner. It isn't on the busy main street, so it's quite a bit quieter than the other stores…"

"To me, that sounds perfect," said Stacy, enjoying

the idea more and more.

"Get right on that then!" said Smithy as the car began to move and she sounded the horn, leaving Stacy with no chance to even say goodbye.

In her hesitation, Stacy wandered up to the main street of the small town. At that time of the morning it was quiet – just as she liked. Walking along the wooden footpath, she smiled to herself. Was she in a town or was she on a movie set? Everything was beyond belief in her new life. After all that she'd been through, how had she now come to be so lucky?

The sound of another car horn made her jump from her thoughts. Looking up, she saw Chad wave and smile at her as he passed, prompting her to return the same. That was another surprising aspect of her life now. They'd only spoken a few times and there was nothing that suggested he had any interest in her romantically, but she couldn't deny it felt nice to have a man smile at her instead of do cruel things to her. She wouldn't read anything into his friendliness – it would take much more than a nice smile and the delicious scent of aftershave to give her the confidence to trust any man again – but it was nice to at least consider she might have met a man who was kind.

When she'd walked the length of the main part of town, she turned to search for the shop Smithy had talked about. Finding it easily, Stacy felt pleased she'd already started to know how to get around the township. Would it be her home forever more, moving forward? She didn't know the answer to that but, certainly for the moment, it seemed a great place to call home.

"Good morning!" she heard a woman's voice say as Stacy approached the store. "Looks like it's going to be a great day!"

As Stacy smiled at the woman, she felt a moment of panic. Over recent years, she'd had it drummed into her that a woman's place was in the home and not in the workforce. For a fleeting moment, her husband's insistence on that rule wanted to take over her growing independent thinking and her confidence. Were his beliefs about that right? Should she have been staying at home, even now, looking after Patti, and the two of them never seeing anyone else? No, she fought against that thinking. She and Patti both needed to interact with other people, and Patti was already proving happy to be in the preschool, playing with other children. No, Ricky's beliefs that a mother should stay at home and *only* ever see her husband and her children were no longer relevant. From now on, only Stacy's thoughts were important. Holding onto that thinking, Stacy finally spoke up.

"I'm Stacy," she said. "I heard that … maybe … you are looking for someone to help out here?"

The smile on the woman's face instantly put Stacy at ease.

"I definitely will need some help over the coming cruise season," she said. "I'm Ella," she added, holding out her hand. "I'm just gonna make a cup of coffee. Want one?"

Minutes later, the two women were sitting on an outside wooden seat that looked, to Stacy, like it might have actually been there since the gold rush days. Sitting there, in the sunshine, sipping the cup of coffee that had been presented to her, she prepared herself for the rejection that might be about to come.

"I haven't had any retail experience, but I am eager to learn," she admitted timidly.

"Well, eagerness to learn is a good start," said Ella, nodding. "Tell me a bit about yourself."

After a happy morning so far, the request instantly plunged Stacy back into the negative world of darkness. She couldn't speak about herself – not her true self or how she'd lived the past few years. How was she ever to truly move forward when it would always be the topic of conversation with every new person she met?

Resolved that she couldn't just go into a panic for the rest of her life as she contemplated that, she took a moment and then answered as best she could.

"I am a single mom," she said. "My little girl, Patti, and I just arrived in Skagway recently to embark on a new beginning – a new chapter."

"A new beginning," said Ella. "Well, Stacy, you might be surprised about just how many people come to this sleepy little town for exactly that reason."

"Really?"

"Oh, yeah," Ella replied, delivering the warmest of smiles. "Your little girl, Patti – is she in school?"

"She's three and she's just started at the preschool here," Stacy said, again feeling a sudden level of nervousness about talking about herself and Patti.

"Oh, she'll love it over there," said Ella. "I have two grandbabies there at the moment, and they yibba yabba all about how much fun they've had when I see them at the weekends. Patti will be fine there too," she added as she patted Stacy's hand. "Now, let's talk about work. You have somewhere for Patti to go during the week. For now, that'd be fine with things so quiet here, but when the cruise season starts, we are open seven days a week for that whole six month period."

"Oh, I see," said Stacy as reality hit. She didn't have any second option for watching Patti - no family and no friends.

"But like I say, my son has two kids who must be around the same age since they're at the preschool too," Ella then said. "So let's not dwell on that too much right now. If the kids are all getting on fine at the preschool, I might be able to twist my daughter-in-law's arm and ask her to watch Patti on the weekends once the season is underway…"

For a moment, Stacy felt panic set in again. Someone she didn't know looking after her daughter? Was that wise? How could she know Patti would be safe? Then she thought about the people she'd met in Skagway so far. She'd met the sheriff; she was getting to know the deputy sheriff; and she'd met one other law enforcement officer who might or might not be staying around for a while. If there was anything bad to find out about Ella's son and his wife, surely Stacy would be told.

"In the meantime," she heard Ella continue. "You said you have no retail experience. Do you think you could enjoy serving people? That might not be the most important aspect of working in a store elsewhere, but in this town it's essential. All store owners here get along well enough even though a lot of us sell similar things, but I do pride myself on trying to provide the passengers who pass through these doors, with the best service possible."

"I think … I mean, right now I'm trying to find my feet again after … but I can learn, and I think I would enjoy interacting with people again," Stacy said, trying to be as honest as she could, without saying very much at all.

She watched Ella study her face for a long while as she sipped her coffee. It was unnerving but all Stacy could do was tell herself that what was meant to be, would be.

"Tell you what," Ella said after what appeared to be a lengthy period of contemplation. "The season doesn't start for another few weeks. Right now I'm open but generally I don't sell as much to the locals as I do to the tourists, so this time, for me, is about making sure the stock is set up, priced right, and ready to sell. If you're up for it, I'm happy for you to come in on Monday and start helping out here. That'd give you some time to become familiar with all the things that I sell, and using the POS machine and what not. It'll also give you and me both enough time, before the rush begins, to suss each other out and see if it can work. How does that sound?"

"I … I don't know what to say," Stacy replied, not able to stop unexpected tears of appreciation beginning.

"Say yes," Ella said. Seeing her then laugh softly made Stacy smile in return. "I can see you're a good girl who perhaps needs a chance. No promises for the long haul, Stacy, but I'm happy for you and me to muddle in for a couple of weeks and see where that takes us."

"That … that sounds perfect," Stacy said. A couple of weeks to see how it goes. That sounded like exactly what she needed – something not so locked in that she'd constantly worry she was letting someone down, but something that she could give her best to and see how it went. "Thank you so much."

"Don't thank me yet," said Ella. "You might hate it!" she added, laughing. "Go and enjoy your day now, and I'll see you at this door at 8.30 Monday morning."

"I'll be here," said Stacy as she stood and reached to take Ella's cup.

"Oh, don't you worry about these. Off you go and have a good day," Ella said again, as if to dismiss Stacy altogether.

Walking away, the familiar uncertainty fell over Stacy again. Feeling it angered her. Had the years of listening to Ricky telling her that a mother shouldn't work actually sunk in so much that she should feel guilty for wanting to get a job to raise her daughter. No! She wouldn't accept that! He had played havoc on her life for long enough. That time – his time – was over!

Wandering around, she felt safe and secure enough to go and get some groceries. She and Patti weren't big eaters, and when she'd been a full time wife her husband had controlled even that, placing orders online for groceries to be delivered to their home rather than risk having Stacy head out and visit the supermarket. Before she'd met him, she'd been independent. Over her time with him, he'd successfully turned her into a zombie who'd lost the confidence to do anything.

Looking at the building that housed the small town supermarket, she took a moment to think about how much cash she actually had. She'd had to leave behind any possible access to any finances in her now-past home. Now she had a small cash budget to work to, for however long it took to start standing on her own two feet. She was grateful that things like that were covered for her escape. She supposed some would look at the small budget and not be happy with the amount of it. All she could do was appreciate it.

Keeping the figure in mind, Stacy lifted her head up high and strode in. She had a brain, and once upon a time she'd been good at math. She could figure out buying groceries for her and Patti, and stick to a budget while doing it. She was sure of it!

Entering the large doors, the larger-than-it-looked-from-the-outside interior made her confidence waver for just a moment before she determined to not let it. There were baskets and there were trolleys. Which to choose? Given that she was walking everywhere, the basket made the most logical sense and won out.

Beginning to work her way through the aisles, it didn't take long to start to feel overwhelmed. There was so much to choose from, but she knew she had to get fruit and vegetables. That was the first place to start in her healing of mind and body.

"Hello again," she heard the now familiar deep voice say from behind her, startling her and prompting her to turn around.

"Oh, hi," Stacy blurted out, more than a little embarrassed that she'd been caught out not knowing exactly what she needed to buy. Who didn't know how to shop in a supermarket?

As Chad watched her and noticed her discomfort, he felt regret at having approached her quite so forcefully. She had things she was recovering from, he was sure. Because of that, he considered he should probably take more care when he approached her in the future but, for the moment, she was already facing him, even if it was with a deer-in-the-headlights expression.

"Sorry, I didn't mean to startle you," he said and saw her begin to relax.

"No, it's … it's okay," said Stacy as she tried to regain her composure. "To be honest, you caught me in a moment of uncertainty. I feel … I feel a little silly, to tell the truth."

"Silly?" Chad asked, intrigued. "Silly in a good way, like childishly happy? Or silly…"

"No, the other version of silly," Stacy said, smiling shyly. It was embarrassing, but it was what it was. "I … I haven't bought groceries for a very long time and I … I know it sounds stupid but…"

"But it's not as easy as it once was," Chad offered and saw her nod.

"Right," said Stacy as she felt her cheeks begin to grow red. Blushing? How could that even happen after all she'd been through? The discovery made her even more flustered and embarrassed.

"Well, I guess you have two choices – buy what you know you like to eat, or buy what you don't know you like to eat but have always wanted to try," Chad said, grinning. "Of course you could also buy what you know you *don't* like to eat, but that option probably *would* be silly!"

Despite the lack of true humor in his words, and the embarrassment she was feeling, Stacy giggled. She giggled and it felt *good.*

"Agreed," she said, enjoying how easy it was to chat to him. They still hadn't said a great deal on their random meetings but there was something very likeable about the man who was friendly but not in any way pushy. It made remaining stress-free a little easier while she found her place in her new home.

"How are you today?" she asked in an attempt to shift the focus away from her internal thoughts.

Recognizing it was the first time she'd asked him that simple question, Chad felt pleased. Sometimes people went through things that kept them inside their own head far too much. Whenever he heard someone like that ask a question about someone other than themselves, he knew it was a sure sign they were finally on the road to healing from whatever trauma they'd experienced.

"Hungry!" he replied, enjoying the smile he again received from her. "I'm just ducking in here to grab something quick before I head back to the office, so won't even look at those healthy options there." Feeling the desire to not make her feel uncomfortable, he just as quickly excused himself. "Best I keep moving. Enjoy those veges!"

As Stacy watched him walk away and move out of sight, she didn't rush to wipe the smile off her face. If nothing else, the short interactions she was having with him and the other people she'd met were certainly at the level of interaction she could handle for the moment. Just enough, and not too much. Perfect.

Wandering around from aisle to aisle, she began to enjoy the process. How had she let Ricky control her so much, she heard in the peace of her mind. Why had she let him dictate that she would stop doing so many things that were just normal for people to do, like go and buy groceries? How had she even justified it all to herself for all of that time? Now, with every day that passed, she felt like she was an outsider, looking at her past self and shaking her head in disbelief. But what was done was done and there was no undoing it. She was fortunate to be in a safe and secure place, with people around her who understood she needed time to grow a new life for her and her daughter. She'd had help to get away from terror and trauma. She knew many never would.

As her mind wandered back again from her past unhappiness to where she currently stood, she thought about Chad Andrews. He kept crossing her path but neither of them had shared anything of real detail with each other. Was he married? Engaged? Attached in any way at all? Did he know that she was in protection by law enforcement? Was that something he would have been told the details of when the police moved her to Skagway, or was he just an escort with no details about her background at all?

So many unknowns. She'd thought it would be hard to get away and start a new life without Ricky but there were many aspects that she hadn't even thought about. Still, she *was* away, and she *was* safe, and life could only get better … surely!

CHAPTER 10

Although his mind continued to threaten that it wanted to think about the woman in the supermarket instead of work, Chad had to push himself to maintain focus. Romance wasn't something he'd had any time for in recent years, and he didn't regard it as something fair to have when he was in the job he was in. There was no point in thinking about it and, even if there was, he could tell Stacy was someone who needed space, not attention.

"Ugh!" he exclaimed to himself as he yet again had to refocus.

"Problem?" he heard a female voice ask from the open doorway of his office. Looking up, he saw the deputy sheriff standing there, smiling at him.

"Just a minor case of thought distraction today," Chad replied. "Nothing for you to worry about, Deputy."

"Woman issues?" Smithy asked as she grinned. She'd met Chad a few times before his current assignment. Although neither had ever been interested in anything happening between them, she knew him well enough to be able to read his moods. "Come on, tell me all about it."

Watching her enter his office and sit down in front of him, Chad couldn't help but smile. Over their years of meeting up now and then on different cases, she'd proven she could be annoying at times, but purely in an 'annoying younger sister' way. He'd seen her move up through the ranks since he'd first met her years earlier, and he could only be happy about that.

"You know I don't do relationships," he said in an effort to make her questioning stop.

"Oh, I know you *think* that," Smithy said. "What *I* think is that even the hardest working cold case detectives need some TLC sometimes. But I can see you're working so I won't give you a hard time…"

"Again."

"Again," Smithy agreed, chuckling. "Seriously though, is there anything I can help with on this case of yours?"

"How much do you know about this one?"

"Only a bit," said Smithy. "I wasn't in town when it happened so I've really only read the same stuff you have. I can't provide anything new other than what's in those boxes."

"Right," said Chad, thoughtful. "Gut instinct, based on what you read?"

He watched as Smithy shrugged her shoulders and grew serious. "I always thought something might have been done to her by someone who didn't live here," she said. "I mean, even though I grew up here before I moved away, I feel like I'm still only just getting to know a lot of the people who live here, and lots who lived here then have now moved on but … I dunno, this is such a … *transient* place, I guess, with the ships coming and going so much over the summer. Most days there's at least one ship in port. That's a *lot* of strangers coming and going."

"Hmm," Chad mumbled, his mind working over possibilities. "Where could someone off a ship have taken Missy though? They couldn't get her *on* the ship, and the ships are here only for a relatively small amount of hours every day…"

"And *that* is why you're a big shot cold case solver, Chad Andrews, while I am only a mere deputy sheriff!" Smithy said as she smiled at him and stood. "But seriously – I know you're here to do a job, and I have no doubt you will do great at this and get the family the answers they deserve, but please do remember sometime that you're also a *man*."

On hearing her words, Chad couldn't help but laugh

at her suggestiveness. On almost every occasion they'd seen each other, she'd teased him about being single. It seemed nothing had changed.

"Get out of here!" he said with sternness in his voice before turning back to his notes. In another life he might have been a husband and a father by now. In this one, people needed him.

CHAPTER 11

The day before she began working at the store on 5th Avenue, Stacy took Patti to the local library. It was the first time they'd visited the small building, but it proved a joy as soon as they walked in. Sitting cross-legged on the floor with her little one happily snuggled into her arms while taking time to turn the pages of the picture books they'd selected, Stacy wondered why life couldn't have always been so happy and easy.

She was enjoying the simplicity of it all when she saw the door to the library open. At first she thought she was seeing things but then she was sure. It was Ricky walking in. Feeling her heart start to pound heavily, she sat still, looking around to see who could protect her.

What could she do? How could she stop him from doing whatever he must surely want to do to her now? With Patti firmly in her arms, she remained where she was, tightly closed her eyes, began to take long, deep breaths in and out, and waited for whatever punishment she was going to have to endure for having moved away and left him.

"Stacy?" she heard the familiar voice ask. It took a long moment for her brain to process the simple one-word question and come to a sharp realization – if it was Ricky, he wouldn't have said her new name. He would have called her Monica. It wasn't him. It *couldn't* have been him.

When she finally opened her eyes, she saw Chad crouching down in front of where she still sat with Patti in her arms. The look on his face told her clearly that he'd seen expressions before that must have been just like the one she'd just shown him.

As she glanced around the library to make sure Ricky really wasn't there, she finally focused fully on the man she'd now and then been chatting to. He was wearing the clothes she'd thought she'd just seen Ricky walk in wearing. Despite understanding her mind had just been mixed up, it took some time and effort for her to get her breathing and heart rate back to normal.

"I'm not him," Chad said, taking a pure guess at what had just set her off in her panic. He had no idea if a man was involved in whatever she'd had to get away from but, reading her face in response to what he'd said, he suspected his guess had been correct. She was on the run from a man – a man who had either hurt her severely, or *could* hurt her severely. "You're okay. No matter who he is, he isn't here."

Stacy maintained eye contact with him, determined to not let her mind play a trick like that on her again. She'd been gone from her previous home for a short time, but it was the first time anything like that had happened. How cruel could the human mind be to play such a trick?

"I'm okay," said Stacy when she felt her body relax. "Thank you. I thought…" she started to add before realizing once again that she couldn't talk about anything to do with … anything.

"You thought you saw someone you desperately don't want to see again," Chad suggested and saw her nod. "You aren't the first to experience what you just did. Unfortunately, in my line of work, I've seen it far too often."

Stacy nodded but held back from asking anything about him. If he wanted to share, she was open to that, even though she knew she never could do the same in return.

"What are you doing here?" she finally asked, feeling it was a safe question to help the awkwardness to pass.

"Well, I came in here to look for books on the

history of this town and the surrounding areas," Chad replied. "But now…"

"Now?"

"Now I wonder if I was drawn to come in here for an entirely different reason," Chad said quietly.

"To play with my head?" Stacy suggested, forcing a shy smile.

"Or perhaps to help you with the games your head is trying to play," said Chad, chuckling.

"Duck!" Patti said, surprising them both as she held up the book she was flicking through and pointed at a page.

The timing of it made Chad and Stacy smile at one another in relief.

"*Are* you okay?" Chad asked one more time.

"Yes, I … yeah, I'm fine," Stacy replied. "Go forth and find your history books. Honestly, I am going to be okay."

"Yes, you are," Chad said before standing and moving away. In part, he wanted to stay by her side and ask her to talk, but he knew that was very against the general rules she'd likely received when she'd been moved. The irony of that wasn't lost on Chad as he considered that he was in exactly the same position as she might be – wishing they could talk about things that laws said they couldn't.

CHAPTER 12

"Nice and early - I like that!" Stacy heard Ella call out on Monday morning. Thoughts of what had happened in the library the day before had plagued Stacy throughout the evening but having the new challenge of Monday morning to look forward to had helped. It had enabled her to actively think about something that was going to happen, that was hopefully going to be a positive thing in the lives of her and Patti both.

Heading to the store earlier than required and sitting down on that old seat outside as the sun moved up in the sky had enabled her to meditate and ease her nerves before her new boss turned up.

"Come on inside," Ella said when she reached the door. "For this week, you won't need to worry about opening up or anything like that, but if you decide to stick around for the cruise ship season, we will cover it just in case I can't make it into work one morning or anything like that. But, for now, first thing I like to do as soon as I get here in the mornings is…"

As soon as instructions started to be delivered, Stacy began to smile. Strict commands to do this and do that – some people might not have liked that at all but it was exactly what she needed to keep her mind focused on anything other than where it usually wanted to return to. History was the past, but it was and always would be there, settled in one's mind. Instructions that were brand new – yes, that was a much healthier place for her mind to go.

"You look like you've always worked here," she heard hours later when the store door opened. Turning around, she saw the deputy sheriff had entered and was grinning.

"She's a good worker, for sure!" said Ella. "I

certainly can't complain about her enthusiasm to learn!"

"I've only just got here," said Stacy, chuckling.

"Ella's a great judge of character, so I'm gonna believe her," Smithy said. "Two good people helping each other out – that's just what I like to see in my job!"

"Doesn't leave much for you to *do* in your job, though, does it, Deputy!" Ella said, surprising Stacy with her attempt at candid wit.

Smithy laughing at the comment made Stacy smile further. "Don't worry about her picking on me, Stacy. She's been doing that all my life!"

Stacy didn't know what the story was there but didn't want to question it. All she could focus on was the two of them both being among the friendliest people she'd ever met.

"Well, I won't hold you up," Smithy said. "I just wanted to see how the first day was going."

Before Stacy could say anything more, the deputy had walked out and closed the door. As always when Stacy had seen Smithy, she felt joy from her welcoming and friendly nature, but also a lingering question of why the deputy sheriff chatted to her so much, and what exactly it was that Stacy would eventually be called to do in the case of her husband.

"Now, how about you and I…" she heard Ella begin again in another round of instructions. The timing couldn't have been better, given where Stacy knew her thoughts were about to spiral to.

At the end of that first day, she felt good. It was the first time in years that she felt she'd contributed to something outside of herself, and she'd gotten to spend an entire day with an adult. The conversation over the day had centered around the store and small talk, with little personal information shared, and that was exactly what Stacy found to be another way to relax and enjoy the experience.

"You've done real good today, Stacy," Ella said before Stacy walked out. "I hope you'll come back tomorrow…" she added with a silent question in the tone of her voice.

"If you're happy for me to return in the morning, I'll definitely be here," Stacy said, grinning. Seeing Ella nod at her, Stacy finally said her goodbye and walked out, switching her mind from working woman mode to mother mode.

"Hello!" she exclaimed as she walked into the preschool and saw Patti run toward her. Scooping her daughter up and holding her tightly, she realized it was the first time ever that she'd been away from Patti for so many hours in one day. For a moment, Ricky's words haunted her again, making her question her choice to work. The expression on her daughter's face forced his words to fade away. "Have you had a fun day, Patti Cakes?"

Seeing the smile and enthusiastic nod from Patti relieved Stacy. She never wanted to do the wrong thing in raising her daughter. Sometimes it was difficult to determine what was wrong and what was right, but when a staff member approached and again said how easily Patti was fitting in, Stacy was relieved.

"For it being her first full day here, she's done great! Absolutely nothing to worry about there," the staff member said. "If you want her to keep coming full time, we're more than happy to have her here."

"Thank you," Stacy said, pulling Patti tight again. "Yes, I'm hopeful the job I've found will continue longer than these few weeks but, at least for now, she'll be coming every day for the full time hours, if that's okay."

Walking out into the sunshine, she smiled to herself as she listened to the chatter about the day. Listening to three-year-old speak was different to listening to an adult talk all day, but it was certainly no less enjoyable.

Yes, things were falling into place very well, and she felt happier than she had in a very long time. Why, then, did it start to feel like the happy bubble she was in, might pop at any moment?

CHAPTER 13

On the last day of her first working week, Stacy was dismissed early, much to her surprise. Overall, it had been a good few days, eagerly taking in whatever Ella had wanted to teach her, and slowly gaining familiarity with the products she would hopefully soon be selling to eager tourists.

"It's a glorious day and I know you said little Patti is in preschool till the end of the day, so why don't you head off and go take some time for yourself," Ella suggested. "You've really helped me out this week. Go and treat yourself somehow."

For a split moment, Stacy wanted to argue. Then she decided to seize the opportunity instead. She loved being a mom and she'd enjoyed every minute of working in the store, but why not go and take some time alone? Was it selfish? Would Patti know and resent her for that? No, of course she wouldn't. She was happy playing with all the other kids. Despite Stacy not wanting Ricky's voice and words to keep ruling any aspect of her life, it just continued to linger, still making her question every decision she made.

"Hey!" she heard when she stepped out of the store and took a moment to consider options.

Looking up, she saw Chad's car stop a little way up the road and then reverse.

"Hey yourself," Stacy called back as she watched him sit still in his car, doing nothing but look at her and smile.

"I've got a couple of hours before I have to attend a meeting," Chad said as Stacy began to cross the road to speak to him. "I thought I might get out for a walk to clear my head. If you're not doing anything, you're welcome to join me."

Stacy smiled. What exactly was happening between them? *Was* it something, or was it just the same as all the other slowly-developing friendships she was embarking upon with people in the small town? Chad hadn't done or said anything to indicate he wanted anything romantic from her, so why did she find herself analyzing his motives so often?

"Okay," she said, desperately wishing all of her thoughts and doubts would just go away.

"Yeah? Okay, awesome. Jump in and I'll park up near the track," Chad said, feeling a small amount of nervousness begin. What was he nervous about? Sometimes he interviewed and chatted to people all day long. There was never anything to be scared of.

Inside the confine of his car, with her settled into the seat beside him, there was silence. Stacy was aware of him being so close to her, with that gorgeous-scented aftershave that he wore, but she also grew aware of the car heading off to an area of town she was unfamiliar with, and in a different direction entirely.

"Where are we going?" she asked, suddenly feeling a familiar emotion of discomfort, blended with a little bit of panic.

Hearing the change in the tone of her voice, Chad turned to look at her. Again he'd overlooked just how much she might have been through before traveling to Skagway. He suddenly felt annoyed at himself for consistently looking at her as if she was a regular person, when he suspected she'd been moved to the small town due to something very serious and very unhealthy.

"Oh, sorry, I thought we could head over the footbridge to where the land meets the water. There's a viewing spot there, but…"

"No, it's okay," Stacy said as she felt her heartbeat increase a little. The fear was there. She didn't want it to be.

"Stacy, I .. I'm happy to go for a walk wherever you feel comfortable," Chad reassured her as he stopped the car and wondered what the best thing to do was.

"No, Chad, honestly," said Stacy. "I'm the one who should be sorry. I … I keep trying to pretend that … some things … never happened, but they did, and it's like I'm being … as silly as it sounds … it feels sometimes like I'm being haunted. I know it makes no sense…"

"Actually it makes perfect sense," Chad replied. "I don't know anything about your history or your past, and I don't *need* to know, but if you're trying to move on from something, I am here for you, at least while I'm in town, and if I do something to make you feel uncomfortable, just come right out and tell me I'm being an inconsiderate idiot, because I really am most of the time."

On hearing his speech, Stacy felt some of her stress begin to melt away again.

"Something tells me you most definitely are *not* an inconsiderate idiot," she said.

"Yes, well we may have to agree to disagree over that point," Chad said, smiling. "However, right now, what would you like to do? If you'd feel better, we can skip the walk and instead go to one of the local cafés … or the Red Onion Saloon … or…"

"No, I think … I think I want to put faith in you," Stacy forced herself to say. "I mean, I've already been in the remote area of the waterfall with you, and you could have done anything to me there…"

"That is very true," said Chad, not entirely sure if she was being serious or not. "Well, listen, that bridge there leads over to a quiet point that I found just the other day. It's peaceful and, just like up at the waterfall, it just felt good to be there. Plus it's a little quieter without the tourists."

"Ella said the busy season doesn't start for a few weeks…"

"Yeah, I heard that too," said Chad as they started to get out of the car. "If what I saw the other day at the Gold Rush Cemetery was quiet, that place sure must get some traffic when it's the busy season! I didn't know so many people liked being near dead people."

Despite her apprehension, Stacy laughed, and that was something she was still getting used to.

"You sure you're okay walking along here?" Chad asked to check one more time.

"Yes, thank you. I'm … I'm all good," Stacy replied as she fell in step beside him. Not all law enforcement staff were good people, she'd heard, but she chose to believe that the one currently leading her to a remote area was.

"Alrighty!" said Chad, relieved. "Let's go."

A short time later, Stacy found herself carefully climbing over rocks, large and small. That in itself was something new for her. She'd clambered over a couple of big ones up near the waterfall. Making her way over the many where they were walking was another experience altogether.

"Oh!" she exclaimed as she slipped on a loose one.

The feeling of Chad's hand naturally reaching out and grabbing her arm to steady her should have made her feel safe and secure. Instead it instantly took her back to the many other times that someone far less nice had reached out and grabbed that very spot on that very arm, not causing a feeling of security, but instead a feeling of intense pain.

Seeing her face change from the surprise of losing her footing, to the look of terror, Chad was quick in his assessment. Holding her arm only long enough to make sure she was steady on her feet again, he then lowered his hand and took a step backwards. As if she'd read his panic on seeing her own, he then saw tears begin in Stacy's eyes.

"I'm never going to be normal," Stacy cried out in disbelief that something so simple and so innocent had caused such a reaction in her so easily. "I can't … I … just can't…"

Before Chad's eyes, he watched her change from being an upright, strong woman, to a woman crouching down as if she wanted to move into the fetal position and not try to live any more. Inside it broke Chad's heart, but he knew better than to focus on himself in that moment.

"Stacy," he said softly as he crouched down beside her. "Hey."

Waiting for her to regain whatever composure she might want to, he saw her rub at her eyes, trying to hide her tears, and then look at him. Whatever she'd needed or wanted in that moment, he would have happily given her to help take away any of the pain that was obviously well settled inside of her. When he saw her move toward him and then close to him in silent request for him to put his arms around her, he happily but carefully obliged.

Feeling his arms envelope her, Stacy tried to force the fear from within her. He wasn't Ricky, and she knew that. Maybe Chad might turn out to be a similar kind of person that Ricky was, but at some point she had to try and trust people again. If she couldn't do that, what kind of life was she going to be living for the rest of her days?

Closing her eyes, she didn't move to put her arms around him, but focused on how it felt to be held with little possibility of being hurt. She didn't excuse her desire for him to hold her, and she didn't move away in any hurry. With each second that passed, she felt a little bit stronger, and that was exactly what she needed.

"Thank you," she finally said when she slowly pulled back. "It's not easy for me to let someone do that."

Chad nodded but didn't reply. He couldn't ask questions and he knew that, but he equally knew that if she wanted to talk – even in a no-specific-detail roundabout way – about what she'd lived through, he wanted her to feel safe enough to do that.

"I think I'm okay now," Stacy said when she felt fully relaxed again. "Sorry. Do you want to keep walking forward?"

"Yeah," Chad said as he helped her up. For the following minutes, as they continued to carefully walk over the rocks and stones, he watched her but didn't ask anything.

"That looks like a nice spot to sit," he heard Stacy say after a few more minutes. "What do you think?"

"Perfect," Chad replied, trying to sound as normal as he could. It was always a challenge in his job, constantly reading people to know when to encourage them to talk, and when to sit back and just wait to see if they wanted to initiate conversation. She wasn't someone he had to interrogate, but he found himself using the same skills to read her nonetheless.

Settled beside each other on a large flat rock looking out across the bay, both were silent for some time, each in their own thoughts. As Stacy stared out, listening to the tiny ripples of waves lap against the shoreline, she again felt a level of peace she'd never experienced before moving to Skagway. It felt surreal to experience the peace when only moments earlier she'd again been in a panic about something bad happening to her. Would she ever be normal again? *Ever*?

"I do love it here," she finally said quietly as she tried to visualize one day being in a constant state of calm and normality again. "This is the first place I've ever spent any time at all in this kind of environment."

"Yeah?" Chad asked, suddenly remembering something she'd said to him on their travels to the small town. "But you've been here before?"

"Yep, a while back, but only for the day, and I hardly saw anything here then. No, it was always the city for me, as far as choice of place to live goes," Stacy continued. "What about you? Would you say you are more of a city boy or a country boy?"

Chad smiled at her, relieved that the previous stress had seemed to leave her, at least for the moment. "I grew up in the country as a kid, but moved to a city as soon as I left school," he said.

"You've lived in both then," said Stacy. "Which do you prefer?"

"Oh, I think that everywhere has some kind of attraction to it," said Chad. "Certainly with these years where my career has been so important to me, the city provides more opportunities for growth and challenges, but…"

Hearing his hesitation to finish whatever he was going to say, Stacy prompted him to continue. "But?"

In response to her question, she was presented with a smile that she could only describe as beautiful. He'd smiled at her a fair bit since she'd first met him, but that smile was something else. It looked like not just a smile that someone gave because they should, or to make another person feel better, but a true smile that came from true happiness. That kind of smile, she could still only dream of experiencing herself.

"But life is passing and none of us know when our last day will be," Chad said. "Do I want to be living in the middle of a big city when I'm older and retired? To be honest, I don't think I do."

"It is certainly calming being here. Would you move somewhere like this for retirement, do you think?" Stacy asked, appreciating that conversation was about someone other than herself at that moment.

Again, she was presented with a smile that almost

took her breath away. Was he smiling just out of happiness, or was he smiling because of something to do with how he was feeling about her? And if that was the case, how should she feel about it?

"This place is pretty quiet," Chad replied, chuckling. "But as I sit here, now, with you … I don't know. I think that the peace has to be good for me. Too often I see things… things that I need to find a way to de-stress from, and the city can add to stress but it also can provide a lot of distractions that can actually *help* with the stress."

"It's hard to deal with the stress of darkness inside of our heads," said Stacy. "How do you cope with it and not let it affect you?"

"Oh, lots of things definitely do affect me," said Chad. "I don't think I'd be human if they didn't."

"But you always look so happy," Stacy said. "You smile a lot!"

"At you, I do," Chad dared to say as he grinned at her again.

As much as Stacy wasn't sure she wanted to acknowledge it, the sudden feeling of being flirted with hit her hard. Despite a moment of uncertainty about what that actually meant, or how she should feel about it, she couldn't stop herself from grinning right back.

"Thank you," she said after a long moment of silence between them.

"Thank me? For what?"

"For … for everything," she replied. "You've already done so much, escorting me all the way here…"

"Stacy, escorting you to Skagway was part of my job and you know it," Chad said quietly.

"Yeah, I know but … but is *this* part of your job too?"

"Sitting here with you?" Chad asked and saw her nod in response. "No, not at all! I'm just enjoying

getting to know you. These little moments you and I
have now and then are refreshing. You are like …
sunshine in my day."

Hearing the cheesy remark prompted Stacy to
giggle. Everything was mixed up and everything was
confusing, but it still felt very good being able to have a
good laugh.

As Chad watched her giggling, he realized how
much he really had started to enjoy getting to know her.
Maybe they hadn't told each other a great deal about the
big important stuff, or shared the worst stories they
could with each other, but when they were together, they
seemed to be able to relax and gain a unique type of
peace from each other. Wasn't that what he'd always
thought the basis of a good relationship should be? For
people to be themselves even when around someone else?

"Everyone in this town has been so nice," Stacy
said as she looked out over the water. "This isn't your
first visit here, right? I thought you indicated on the
flight that you'd been here before."

"I have been here before, but only for a very short
time," Chad replied. "It was for another case but I didn't
have to be here for as long as I'm expecting to be this
time."

"Oh," said Stacy, pretty sure she couldn't ask him
about the specifics of the case he was working. Did it
have something to do with her? Or Ricky? Was that the
real reason why he was spending time with her – not to
get to know her, but instead gather information about her
husband?

As if a switch was activated inside of her, Stacy
suddenly felt sick. She'd been enjoying getting to know
a few people around town. Were *any* of them actually
being nice to her because they were friendly and truly
wanted her and Patti to feel welcome, or were they all
playing a part to get information from her that would

later be used, whenever she was going to be called in to do whatever it was that law enforcement were going to expect her to do? Although the thought began only as a very slight consideration, it quickly took root and grew from an instant of wonder to a full-on panic attack.

"Stacy?" Chad asked when he watched her facial and body expression all change from seeming to be happy, to tensing up to a similar degree that he'd seen her do previously.

"In your job, how do you ever know who's telling the truth, and who's lying?" Stacy asked as she began ruminating on the possible motives of everyone who'd seemed welcoming to her since she'd arrived in the small town. "I mean, that's part of your job, right? To figure out who's honest and who's a liar?"

As Chad watched her and listened to her questions, he felt slivers of both relief and despair flow over him. He'd met a lot of different kinds of people during his lifetime, and usually he was quick to figure people out, but he couldn't deny there were aspects of his time spent with Stacy that concerned him.

"It *can* be part of my job to try and figure those things out," he said quietly. "On the whole, I think the vast majority of people are honest and good but, yes, in my career I do interact with some who definitely aren't." He paused and watched as she turned her head and looked directly into his eyes. Although she didn't say anything in that moment, she certainly looked as though she was bursting to ask something. "What made you ask that?" he asked, hoping she would speak her truth of that moment so they could both relax again.

"Are you getting to know me, just for me, Chad, or is there another reason you're hanging out with me?" Stacy dared to ask. She knew the question could as easily be answered with a lie as it could with an honest answer, but at least she would be able to see his face as he answered.

"I don't have any ulterior motive," Chad replied, making sure to keep watching her face. He had no idea what was going on in her thoughts, but people not trusting him was, unfortunately, something that came with the territory of being in law enforcement. "What's on your mind?"

"Do … do you know why I came to Skagway?" Stacy pushed.

"No," Chad said as he maintained eye contact with her. "I have no idea what was going on with you on that day. I was there because I'd already been assigned to come here and look into the disappearance of someone, and me traveling here fitted in with the police wanting to bring you here at the same time. Whatever reason you've come here for, I haven't been told anything about it, Stacy. Honest."

Stacy nodded but decided to keep an open mind, fully resigned to the possibility that never again in her life would she ever feel like she could trust anyone.

"Look, you never have to tell me what happened to you before coming here, but I hope you know that you can be open with me about what *is* happening with you," Chad said as he reached out and took her hand in his. "I've been in law enforcement for a long time, so seeing people in distress, and nervous … and scared … that's all part of my job and you won't freak me out or anything like that if you have panic attacks or…"

"Freak outs," Stacy said, trying to smile. "That's what I've been thinking of them as. I don't really understand what happens. It's like I'm feeling content and happy for the first time in a long time, and then my brain just switches – almost as if it doesn't *want* me to be happy."

"And maybe that *is* what's happening at those times," said Chad.

"But why would our own brains make that kind of decision, to prevent the feeling of happiness from staying around?" asked Stacy.

"Because brains are weird," Chad said, chuckling. "I know it makes no sense but our minds can be our own worst enemy so much of the time. Honestly, there's no shortage of people who can hear their own brain abusing them – putting them down and not letting them be confident in who they are. Yeah, it's rough, and it's an incredibly stupid thing for the mind to do, but it does happen to, I think, a huge portion of the world's population. That may not be the same as what you're experiencing, I know. If I'm right in thinking something horrible has actually happened to you…" Seeing her nod pushed Chad to continue. "Have you been offered some kind of counseling? I mean, is that something you would want to go through?"

"I think my default plan is to just try and forget it," Stacy replied, taking her time to really tune in and feel what it was like to have a kind man holding her hand. When had that last happened? Did it *ever* happen with Ricky? She supposed it must have, way back at the start. She'd married him, after all. Somewhere in the mix there had been happiness, although her mind currently seemed set on making her forget the good times. "It isn't a good plan, I'm starting to think, but I am happy here, and I need to believe that as time passes, I'll have these … weird things happening … less and less." Hearing no reply but knowing he was looking at her intently, Stacy lifted her eyes from the slow caressing of his hand against hers, and met his gaze. "Do you think that's the wrong way for me to approach this?" she asked.

As Chad heard the question, his heart felt for her. Even now, after whatever had happened to her that had caused her to be whisked away from her previous home by law enforcement, there might still be a part of her that wanted some kind of validation and reassurance that she was saying and doing the right thing. That was a sure sign of her having been heavily controlled by someone, and something Chad had seen far too often in his years of work, especially from women victims. It was also something he hoped Stacy would be able to move past with time to come.

"I think you can have faith in the fact that you are a strong woman, and you will find the way forward that's best for you and Patti," he said as he lifted his free hand and gently moved stray strands of hair from her face. "Maybe there's no right way to do anything, or any wrong way. Whatever you've come here to escape from, you're already being amazing as a mother who loves and cares for her child, and allowing both of you to meet people and make new friends. You're doing great. Believe in that, and believe in yourself. I do."

As he watched her appear to consider what he'd said, he remained quiet, allowing her to process whatever thoughts were flowing over her mind at that moment. After a long period of silence, he saw her lift his hand to her lips and kiss it. Surprisingly, at that moment, Chad felt something he hadn't felt for a very long time – desire. Not just sexual desire, but a desire to know her so much better than he did, while respecting whatever boundaries she wanted to place on them getting to know each other.

Despite the importance his body instantly placed on wanting to move closer to her, not only emotionally but also physically, he remained still. Another woman, he might have kissed. It felt like the right time and place for that, but he just couldn't – wouldn't – give in to bodily desire with Stacy. He'd known her such a short time but couldn't deny there was something connecting them - something powerful that was yet to be investigated. Even so, no matter how powerful it was, he wouldn't let it be just a physical connection.

As Stacy sat and studied his eyes, she also felt a strong pull toward him. What was she supposed to do with that? It had been so long since she'd had any loving or nice physical interaction with a man – even the man she'd married, who was still her husband even though she hoped she would never have to interact with him again after the way he'd treated her. Even considering that – the fact that she was still married – played with her emotions. It wasn't right to not be faithful to the man she'd married, but yet how had he behaved toward her? All the days he'd spent away from the house, had *he* been faithful to *her*? There had been times when she'd secretly hoped he would find someone else and want to get a divorce, but if he had found anyone else, he'd never shared that information with Stacy. Where she sat as far as married went, the line was too hazy to try and figure out.

She'd almost convinced herself that nothing romantic could ever happen between her and Chad – nothing could happen between her and *any* man. Then she looked into his eyes again, and felt what she hadn't felt for far too long. She was attracted to him – to his kindness and to his physical self. She was attracted to him emotionally and physically and, although she did constantly feel like she'd become just one huge ball of confusion, she hoped he was equally attracted to her too.

Without any further thought, she made a decision and slowly leaned in toward him. She hoped he wouldn't reject her but, if he did, she would accept that. As she moved closer, she gave pause to see if he would pull away. He didn't. When her lips touched his, she remained aware that she could be making a mistake that would instantly end what was beginning to feel like the formation of at least a new friendship. There was fear inside of her, but she didn't pull away. Instead she relished the initial surprise that she could sense in him. Then she relished the way his lips started to move against hers, first tentatively and then with far more initiative.

Pulling away after that first exploration, they looked at each other in silence. It took quite some time before either one of them fully processed what had happened enough to be able to speak.

"I liked that," Stacy finally said as she blushed. Inside, she still felt the same conflicts she always did, but she couldn't deny how good she felt at the same time.

"Me too," Chad agreed as he grinned and lifted her hand to his lips. "A lot."

Instead of trying to think of something to say, Stacy turned her glance out toward the water, took some deep breaths, and indulged in her new appreciation for simply being in nature.

"I need to go and pick up Patti soon," she finally said.

"And I need to go and do some more work," said Chad. "I'll give you a ride to the preschool if you like."

Stacy smiled as she accepted his offer to help her up off the large rock they'd been sitting on. Neither said anything more about the kiss they'd shared, or what it could mean, and she was quite okay with that.

CHAPTER 14

The following Monday, Stacy arrived at work early to once again enjoy the morning sunshine beaming down on the old wooden seat outside the store. It had been a quiet weekend, mostly spent relaxing at home with Patti, intermingled with the small walks they'd done together. Several times she'd found herself daydreaming as she remembered the kiss she'd shared with Chad. The memory lingered, along with a burning curiosity about whether he might have been thinking about it as much as she had, or if kissing women might be something so common for him that he wouldn't have given it another thought.

"You look happy today," she heard Ella say as she approached. "What a smile! Does that mean you're pleased to be working here?"

"Absolutely!" Stacy said, with no desire to hide her grin. "I enjoyed last week, and I appreciate you giving me this opportunity, Ella."

"Oh, nonsense," Ella said. "It's you helping me, not me helping you!"

As she opened the door, the two women chuckled together before getting on with the day's chores, as if they'd been working together for years.

With the store being as quiet as Ella had initially implied it would be, Stacy felt fortunate. She'd needed to find work so that she could start to truly rebuild her life as mother to Patti, but she knew she didn't have the confidence to deal with large groups of people. She hoped that would come, but she equally knew she wasn't there yet. On each of the days she'd been helping in the store, a handful of customers had strolled in at most, and that was just enough to help Stacy to begin settling back into being a working woman.

Towards the end of the day, she found herself starting to daydream about that kiss again. She hadn't seen Chad over the weekend. Was he thinking about her as much as she was thinking about him? She was deep in thought about that when someone walking into the store changed the feeling of joy to one of terror.

"Stacy?" she heard Ella ask through what felt like a haze in Stacy's brain. The words were reaching her, but they weren't dispelling the feeling of terror she felt as she gazed at who had just walked in.

"Excuse me," she then heard the man say in an attempt to get the attention of Stacy or Ella. It was a voice that she knew well – far *too* well – and yet…

It was then, when the man approached the counter and was standing directly in front of Stacy, that her brain finally acknowledged he was a man she'd never laid eyes on before. It wasn't Ricky, like she had instantly thought. It wasn't Ricky, her husband. It was just a regular guy, asking about a product that was for sale. He wasn't who she'd thought he was, and he wasn't there to hurt anyone.

"Yes, how can I help?" she heard Ella ask the man as she moved from behind the counter to direct him away so she could help him.

Stacy experienced a mixture of emotion as she felt fear flow out of her and slowly be replaced with relief, but also intense sadness. In the silence of her mind, she heard the same old question that kept hitting her over and over, no matter how many ways her life was getting better and healthier: would she ever be normal? Since arriving in her new home, she'd asked that very question far too many times.

Seizing the moment to duck out to the store's small storeroom, she tried as hard as she could to not cry. She was in a workplace where she could only hope she might be able to have a secure future with a secure income. She didn't want Ella to see what a mess she was. If that happened, she would surely lose her job and, along with it, any shred of confidence she'd started to gain.

"Stacy," she heard Ella's voice call out from the other side of the door minutes later. "Stacy, it's okay. The customer has gone. Come out and talk to me."

As much as Stacy wanted to remain where she was and just hide from Ella and the rest of the world, she knew she couldn't. She'd managed to stop the flow of tears that wanted to break forth, but they were still there, pushing to break free.

Slowly opening the door, she took a deep breath and prepared to try and look normal. The expression on Ella's face – one of concern but also of care – finally broke the tears free in a torrent.

"Oh you poor thing," Ella said as she opened her arms and welcomed Stacy into them. "Let yourself have a good cry and then come and sit down outside in the sun. I'll make us a cup of coffee. You don't need to tell me anything – just take some time to let the tears all out, until they've run their course."

"Thank you," Stacy said, seizing the opportunity – and the permission – to cry as hard and for as long as she needed to. Between either being at home with Patti and not wanting to cry in front of her, and equally not wanting to cry in public, maybe it had been too long that she'd been trying to hold everything in. Yes, she'd cried, but she'd always tried to keep it quiet and hidden, and cut it short as soon as she could. Was that really working for her? She knew the answer to that silent question was a resounding 'no!'.

When she finally felt the tears naturally dry up, she moved to the small staff bathroom and splashed water on her face. It wouldn't do anything to stop the redness of her eyes or her face, but it still felt refreshing, and just really, really good. After taking a long time to look in the mirror and wish she hadn't cried in front of the woman who could have become her full-time boss, Stacy heard Ricky's words – his rule – all over again. Women shouldn't be in the workplace. They should be at home, and *only* at home.

"Screw you!" she called out into the mirror, not at herself but at the ghostly presence of her husband that she always thought she could feel around her – even now. "You don't control me any more!"

"You okay, Doll?" Ella asked when Stacy finally walked out into the sunshine.

"Yeah, although a bit embarrassed…" Stacy replied.

"Embarrassed? Oh, no, don't you ever be that!" said Ella as she handed Stacy the warm cup. "Things happen in our lives that push us to our limits sometimes, and no matter how hard we want to forget them, it's almost impossible to. And don't be embarrassed about crying either. We all need to do it sometimes, and it's therapeutic to do it. Do you feel better, having let it all out?"

Stacy nodded and smiled sadly. As annoyed as she was that it had happened when and where it had, she could only agree that having cried until she had no more tears in her, had left her with an incredible feeling of calm.

"Of course you do!" Ella said. "Nothing to be embarrassed about at all."

"But the customer…" Stacy started to say, dreading what was to come.

"He's alright," Ella reassured her as she patted Stacy's hand. "And so will any others that ever come in when you feel like that, although I suspect that as we get busier, you'll find your mind thinking about anything other than work, less and less."

"You … you're not … firing me then?" Stacy asked, wanting it to be over with quickly if it was coming at all.

In response she saw Ella laugh out loud as she patted Stacy's hand again. "I am not! You have already proven how good a worker you are. If you're happy to stay on and ease into the busy season with me, I'm happy to have you."

"It wasn't my thoughts that took over then, Ella," Stacy said quietly. "It was the man…"

"If I'm guessing right, he looked like someone you used to know," Ella surmised and saw Stacy nod. "It can certainly happen, and with the numbers coming through in the few months to come, there might be a lot more people who look like whoever you're trying to leave behind and forget."

"If that happens again, it isn't really fair to you … or them!"

"Let's just face that challenge if it happens," said Ella. "For now, you had a scare and you had a cry, and now you feel better, yes?"

Stacy nodded. Yes, she certainly did feel better, despite how much terror the incident had caused in her only minutes earlier.

"Good!" Ella said. "Now, then, let's sit here and enjoy this fine coffee I made, and the fresh air and sunshine, and then we'll get back into it. Yeah?"

"Yes," Stacy agreed. "Thank you, Ella."

"You're a good girl," said Ella quietly. "There are many people in this town who've come here to escape one thing or another, so don't worry. We all understand that we all have pasts and, sometimes, no matter how much we want to keep those pasts to ourselves, they do come back now and then to haunt us. You aren't the first one I've met here with a ghost, and you won't be the last, but you are still a good worker and together we're going to get you through this."

Feeling calm again, Stacy turned and embraced the older woman. She would never want to share anything about what she'd let Ricky do to her over their time together, but she appreciated knowing that she wasn't the only one in town who had a past to hide.

"Right, back to work we go!" Ella called out as she stood, indicating the moment of seriousness was over, at least for the moment.

CHAPTER 16

As Chad sat at his desk on that Monday, he found his thoughts drifting back to a certain kiss he'd shared a few days earlier. It wasn't convenient, and it was hardly professional, but it still remained on his mind.

What was it that made that kiss – and Stacy herself – linger in his thoughts so much? He wanted to reject it as being something he shouldn't be paying attention to, but that was definitely proving easier said than done. The fact was that the woman he'd escorted to Skagway weeks earlier had made an impression on him and he was truly enjoying getting to know her. Was that something he should be scared of? Usually, on the rare occasion that someone did capture his attention as much as Stacy had, Chad wanted to cool things off, and quickly. A relationship was something he didn't feel he could or should offer anyone. Did he want to cast aside the feelings he was developing for Stacy, quite so easily?

"Hey, how's it all going?" he heard Smithy's voice ask as she entered the small office he'd claimed as his own for the duration of his investigation.

"There's a lot to go through," Chad replied, glancing at the boxes that he'd still only read about two-thirds of the contents of. "I've talked to almost everyone who was living in town at the time, and is still here. I'll be heading off this time next week to go and chase up some others who now live out of town."

"You'll be leaving?" Smithy asked as she sat down on the other side of the desk.

"Only for as long as it takes for me to go do some questioning," Chad said, smiling at her. "You gonna miss me?" he added, teasing her.

Smithy laughed softly. Since she'd first met him, they'd fallen into a pattern of teasing each other and she liked that. He was someone she imagined would have been a great big brother – or, to the right person, a great partner.

"Of course," she replied. "Seeing your ugly face always makes my day!"

Chad laughed as he watched her move to stand up, and then turn to look at him with a more serious expression on her face.

"Get the bastard who did this," she said.

"You sound certain that (a) something serious has definitely happened to Missy; and (b) it was a guy who did it," Chad said. It was the same assumption he'd come up with too, just as it seemed to be of all the people he'd talked to so far about Missy's disappearance.

"Well, (a) yeah I do think something horrible happened to her and I don't expect she's still alive; and (b) yeah, I think it would definitely be a guy that did it," said Smithy.

"Not all evil people in this world are men," Chad said, briefly thinking about some of the cases he'd worked that had certainly proven to him just how evil women could also be.

"No, but I have a feeling about this one, and it's a guy," Smithy said before suddenly changing her serious look to one of teasing again. "Now stop chatting up this town's deputy and get back to work!"

Despite their serious exchange moments earlier, Chad laughed as he watched her walk out. He couldn't argue with Smithy's summary of what she thought might be the situation with Missy. It was what the general population thought, but was it true? With not having found a body, the idea of her having been taken but still be alive couldn't entirely be eliminated, and neither could the possibility of her having left on her own to simply start a new life away from all who'd known her. His experience told him that was less likely, especially with how many people had said she was a family person and didn't seem to have any grievances with anyone in the town, but there was still that chance…

Once again his mind flipped from the seriousness of the case, back to that kiss…

Shaking his head and smiling to himself, Chad looked down at the page he was currently reading and refocused. Meeting a woman and feeling those moments of being truly alive, and passionate about someone, were things to be rejoiced, but not when a young woman was still missing and her family were still waiting to know what had happened to her.

CHAPTER 17

With each day that passed during her second week of work, Stacy felt her confidence increase. Each time she looked at Ella and heard her talk about one item or another that was sold in the shop, she felt blessed that she'd learned about the position, and that she was being given a chance. Surely not all employers were so generous.

"From next week, things will slowly start getting busier," she heard Ella say when they were both getting ready to shut up shop for her final day of the week. "Don't panic – for all of the years I've been doing this, there's been a slow but steady increase of customers wandering in here from the day when the ships start to arrive. Because we're off the beaten path a bit, we won't get the full-on onslaught that the shops on the main street will, but it will certainly slowly get busier as the days pass."

Stacy felt nervous at the thought of serving lots of people at once, but she also knew that Ella had done a great job of not only telling Stacy about the products for sale, but also quizzing her at different times about those items. Although a little scared about the numbers of customers that might come in, she was sure she'd done pretty well in learning and remembering what each product was, where it had been made and from what, and what the prices and specials were going to be.

"And little Patti is already getting on really well with my grandbabies, so that should work well too," Ella said. "My daughter-in-law loves her already."

Stacy smiled. She and Patti had gone to Ella's son's home in the past weekend and spent some time there so all could see how the kids got on, and how Patti got on with Ella's daughter-in-law. There was certainly an element of concern over leaving Patti with people neither of them knew, but Stacy had quizzed Smithy when she'd run into her. The deputy sheriff hadn't had anything negative to say about Ella, her son, or her daughter-in-law. That was about all that could be done to do any kind of check on who Patti was going to be left with for the two days of each weekend, and Stacy had to just hope it would all work out well.

"Thank you for helping with that too, Ella," Stacy said. "I don't know what I would have done if..."

"Oh, we would have worked something out, even if it was you bringing little Patti in here and working only half days," Ella replied. "But let's see how this goes. It's a long six months, working almost every day in here, but whenever things are quiet, you'll be able to slip away."

"I am looking forward to seeing how Patti goes on the weekends, and how *I* go in the store next week," Stacy said.

"You are going to be just fine," said Ella as she delivered one of her now-regular hand pats. "Now, all is quiet here and we are fully set up for being a bit busier on Monday, so run off and take some time to relax and put your feet up while you can."

Stacy grinned and nodded, noticing how early it was in the day, and seizing the opportunity to go for a walk up to the waterfall.

"Actually I think I might head up to the falls," she said. "Would you like to come?"

The response she got was Ella throwing her head back and laughing as if she'd heard the funniest joke ever.

"Me? Walk all the way up there?" Ella asked. "Thank you, Stacy, but no, I haven't been up there for years! I do remember how lovely it was though. No, you go and enjoy the solitude that it can provide. I don't go there now but I do remember how magical it was when I was younger. Now get out of here and enjoy!"

With no more encouragement needed, Stacy smiled as she walked out into the sunshine. It wasn't a busy or noisy walk once she was clear of the main part of town. The couple of times she'd walked up there since her first visit with Smithy, she'd found the silence away from the township too quiet due to its remoteness. Each time she crossed the train line and got closer to the cemetery, she felt her apprehension change into calmness. Just like Ella had described, it was somewhat magical.

Entering the darkness of the area of bush and trees of the cemetery, she saw a small tour group standing around a grave. The tour operator was so animated in delivering his speech about local scoundrels and the town's history that Stacy grinned at him. It was a quaint little town but she did love that it had quite a big history.

Quietly, taking only a minute or two to listen to the tour operator's words, Stacy edged around the group and began to walk toward the high-falling flow of water.

As with her previous visits, the first step back into the sunshine, combined with the beauty of the water flowing down, momentarily took Stacy's breath away. Looking around, she could see nobody was nearby, inspiring her to stand still for a long time, breathing in the fresh air while absorbing the sounds around her. She'd rejected everything about nature for so much of her life. Standing right in the middle of it, she felt saddened by that. What had kept her in cities all of her life? What had been the attraction of the noise, the overcrowding, and the inability to truly relax there? Had it all been for one person who couldn't have even loved her?

Pushing memories aside again, she moved toward a large rock she'd sat on before. Perched on the side of the waterfall, she relished the feeling of the misty water spray hitting her face. She supposed some would have found it cold and annoying. She only found it refreshing.

Glancing at her watch, she saw she had a couple of hours before she'd have to leave to go and pick up Patti from preschool. Allowing for the walk back, she had plenty of time to sit still, close her eyes, and appreciate the calm she felt over body and her mind. Ideally, she looked forward to the day when she could stay in her present level of calm at all times but, for the moment, being able to have even snippets of peace was enough to start with.

She'd been enjoying the quiet of the environment for quite some time when she heard the now-very-familiar voice speak.

"Hi," Chad said tentatively when he laid eyes on her.

"Hey!" Stacy exclaimed, surprised but smiling. "What … how come you're up here?"

Her surprise prompted Chad to grin broadly. He hadn't seen her since the day they'd kissed, and he'd felt conflicted all week about whether it would cause her more stress to not hear from him, or more stress if he didn't give her space. The smile on her face gave him hope that she was happy to see him.

"Actually I came to see you," Chad admitted. "I called into Ella's store and she said she thought you might be coming this way."

Although Stacy was surprised, she kept quiet. She'd thought about him so much during the week that she could feel her cheeks heat up, indicating she was probably blushing. She supposed she could have been proactive and sought him out over the days that had passed since she'd last seen him, but it had taken time for her to consider all possibilities about what exactly that kiss had meant.

"Would you like some company?" Chad asked, seeing her thoughtfulness.

"Yeah, of course," Stacy replied as she moved over on the large rock she felt she'd claimed as her own. "Is everything okay?"

"Yep," Chad replied as he sat down. Inside of his mind was the uncertainty about whether he should kiss her or not. Would that be nice for her, or would it freak her out? After consideration, he looked closely at her, saw her smile, and decided to take the plunge, again enjoying just how good their lips moved together. "Even better now," he added as he pulled away. "How are you going?"

"I'm good," said Stacy. "What's up that made you want to find me today?"

"Well," Chad began as he reached out and took her hand in his and then raised it to his lips. "I wanted to let you know I'm heading away on Monday, for work…"

"Ahh, it's that time already," Stacy said, feeling intense sadness deep in her heart.

"It's not permanent," Chad said. "It could be a couple of weeks, or it could be just a few days, depending on how things go, but I wanted you to know so you didn't think I just disappeared on you."

Stacy nodded without certainty about what she should say or how she should react. So little had happened between them, but in some ways it definitely felt like *something*.

"All week I've been thinking about our last time together, and that kiss," Chad said. "I haven't tried to see you since because I wasn't sure if you'd want to see me or not, but it's important to me that you know how much I am enjoying getting to know you, and spending time with you. Don't think that if I'm not seeking you out, it's because I don't want to see you," he added. "I love my job, but sometimes it can seem like a curse."

"Why do you say that?" Stacy asked. "You help people. You helped me!"

"Yeah, and I love that aspect of the job, when it works out that I *have* helped someone," Chad said. "It's not always the way, unfortunately, but I have to try and do my best to bring some closure to people if I can. That's why I love working cold cases. Sometimes it can feel to families that there's no hope of finding out what happened to someone important to them. If I can help solve that unknown question, it's certainly worth all the time and effort put into that, but…"

"But?" Stacy asked. The first response she got was a sad smile from the man sitting close to her. The second response was him leaning toward her and gently placing his lips on hers.

"But it does stand in the way of other important aspects of life sometimes," Chad finally said.

"I haven't heard you mention … a … significant other," Stacy dared to say. Both of them had avoided such an obvious thing to know before embarking on any kind of romantic interaction, with both of them having kept quiet. "Are you…" she started to ask before reassessing if she did want to know the answer.

"I wouldn't have let us kiss if I was in any kind of relationship, Stacy," Chad said, grinning. "So, in response to what I think you were about to ask, I am most definitely single."

Although he saw her smile sadly at him, the fact that she didn't provide any information about her own relationship status told Chad that she might be still attached. Did he want to probe about that? He knew that she'd been swept away from someone, alone with only her daughter. Didn't that say enough if she was actually in some kind of relationship?

"Relationships aren't all they're cracked up to be anyway," Stacy said quietly as she diverted her gaze to the waterfall. "You think, when you meet someone, that they're your prince or princess. Then reality hits and you realize there are no princes or princesses. You just fooled yourself into believing there were."

"Stacy, if you do want to share anything…"

"Thank you, but I don't," Stacy said, shutting down the possibility. "You said you don't know why I've come to Skagway, but in your work I'm assuming you'd at least *guess* why I was escorted here by you and the other officer." Pausing for a long while, she saw him nod even though he remained quiet and didn't ask any question. Holding his hand tightly in hers, Stacy looked at him again. "I have – had – a life elsewhere, that still feels uncertain. I'm enjoying this time with you, but I can't make any promises. Everything is just so … *messy*!"

"No promises then," said Chad. "I like hanging out with you. Even seeing you here, like this, makes me happy. I don't need anything more, and next week I'm leaving for a while anyway."

"I hope you come back," Stacy said as she relaxed back.

"I'll be back," Chad reassured her. "I never know for how long I'll be in one place, but I'll definitely be back."

Stacy nodded, smiled, and then gladly welcomed another kiss from him. Neither of them were in any position to offer anything big, or even anything certain, but it was still a nice reprieve from her ongoing thoughts and concerns to receive a warm and safe kiss from a man she was very much growing a physical attraction to.

CHAPTER 18

"Will I see you again before you go?" Stacy asked as she began to walk down from the waterfall area with Chad by her side.

"I'm still here for the weekend," Chad replied, suddenly feeling an unexpected thud in his heart at the thought of leaving Skagway and not knowing exactly how long he would be away.

"I have to work both days of the weekend," said Stacy.

"Well, maybe you would like to bring little Miss Patti over to my place straight after you finish work tomorrow, and let me cook for you both," said Chad.

Hearing him offer to cook a meal surprised Stacy, not because she couldn't imagine him cooking, but because, for far too long, another man had been insisting it was a woman's place in the kitchen, not a man's.

"Yeah?" she asked, not able to stop the grin that wanted to naturally burst forth.

"Yeah," Chad replied, laughing softly at her response. "You won't get anything fancy, I'm sorry to say, but I can hold my own in the kitchen. What do you say?"

"I don't even know where you live…"

"That's easily solved," said Chad as they walked through the cemetery towards where his car was parked. "I can show you now if you like."

"Okay," said Stacy. The mention of seeing wherever his home was made her heart begin to pound. Was that due to excitement, or was it due to fear? She asked herself that question briefly and then just as quickly pushed it aside. She couldn't hide from life forever.

A few minutes later, they pulled up to a small

cottage similar to her own but on the other side of town.

"This is your place?" Stacy asked, realizing she hadn't given any thought to where he might be staying while in the small sleepy township.

"For the duration of my work here, yep," said Chad. "It's nothing flash, but it has everything I need."

Stacy nodded, suddenly aware she was at a man's home. Would he try and get her inside, to do whatever he wanted to her? Would he expect her to give him something that she wasn't sure she could give to any man again after all that she'd been through?

"I promise I'm not going to hurt you in any way, Stacy," Chad said quietly, sensing her sudden tenseness. "Are you comfortable with the idea of you and Patti coming here for a meal tomorrow? If not, I understand. There are plenty of places in town we could eat. We can go out and do whatever you want…"

"No, thank you," Stacy said. "I'm … yeah, I like your first idea. Coming to your home would be really lovely."

"Awesome," said Chad, smiling at the thought of cooking a meal for someone other than himself. It had been quite a while since he'd done that for anyone. "I need to get back to work now for a bit. Can I drop you off somewhere?"

Looking at her watch, Stacy nodded. Inside of her, she felt sadness at the knowledge that the man beside her would be leaving town when they'd just started to know each other. She just had to trust that he was telling the truth and he'd be coming back.

"I'll go and pick up Patti," she said.

"Preschool then," Chad said, grinning as he reversed out of his small driveway and started the journey.

Once at their destination, Stacy turned to glance at him. She'd not considered him in any way handsome when she'd first seen him that day she and Patti had flown away from their previous home. Each time she looked at him now, she was aware of just how much more physically attracted to him she was.

With that thought, she leaned toward him and gave him a kiss that lingered with the growing passion she could feel was waking up inside of her.

"What time tomorrow?" she asked when she finally pulled away and opened the car door.

"A nice and early dinner straight after you finish?" Chad asked. "Like 5pm-ish? Then we can relax for a while afterward, without you worrying about keeping Patti out late. Does that work?"

"Perfect," said Stacy. "See you then."

CHAPTER 19

After finishing work, picking up Patti, and calling into their home the following afternoon, Stacy felt oddly nervous as she readied herself to go to Chad's. It had been many years since she'd had that 'silly girl' feeling – the one that a man could inspire in her. It both excited and scared her. In the eyes of everyone, she was still married. She was still a wife who'd committed to 'till death do us part'. Did she have any right to go to a man's home? To spend time with a man? To kiss a man? Or should she have stayed with Ricky and possibly seen the 'death' part of that vow right through to the end?

No matter what anyone would think, or how they would judge her for what she was currently doing, when she looked at Patti's smiling face, she at least knew she'd done the right thing to get out of that house and tell the police what had been going on.

Getting to know Chad was a side issue, but she couldn't let herself feel bad about what was happening. She wasn't anywhere near ready to sleep with another man, but when she thought about all of the time she'd spent with Chad so far, she couldn't identify any pushiness in him about that. Would the evening to come be different? Could that be the very plan that he had for her when he'd invited her to his house? It could be, but she chose to believe not. He was doing something nice for her, and he was including Patti in that something nice. If she was wrong about his intentions, be it on her head she supposed.

"Right, Patti Cakes," she said, loving the happy grin on her daughter's face. "Shall we go and see what Chad is cooking for us today?"

"Yes!" Patti said as she stood on Stacy's bed and held up her arms to be picked up and held tight.

"Alright then!" said Stacy. "If you want to take one of your favorite books or toys, go and grab it now."

As she put on her jacket, she saw Patti run back to where she stood, with her little backpack in one hand and her favorite stuffed toy in the other.

"Rufus is coming too?"

"He's hungry," Patti said, making Stacy laugh softly as she helped put Patti's coat on.

"Then let's go!"

Walking through the peaceful end of the town, from one side to the other, Stacy looked up and around her. It was mostly green, and the air was cool and fresh, even though summer had officially started. The simplicity and peace of it all, combined with the simple joy that came from holding her daughter's hand as Patti happily skipped along, heightened Stacy's certainty that everything she was doing was right.

"Hey," she heard Chad's voice call out as she and Patti finally embarked up the small path to his front door.

"Hey yourself," she said in reply. Even from the couple of meters away that she was from him, she could smell that delicious scent of his cleanliness and aftershave. "You smell good," she added in a whisper as she passed him in the doorway.

"So do you," Chad said. It was the first time in a very long time that he'd had any woman in any place he'd been staying. To say he was nervous was a huge understatement. "And who is this?" he asked as he crouched down and saw the small dog toy in Patti's arms.

"Rufus!" Patti replied as she held the toy out for Chad to take.

"Hello, Rufus," Chad said, holding the toy briefly before passing him back. "And hello, Miss Patti. Are you hungry?"

Seeing her daughter nod and smile at Chad was a relief to Stacy. A relief but also an initiator of memory –

specifically, the memory of all the times when Patti had smiled at her father … and then been utterly rejected. Although it had never seemed that Patti had been affected by that, continuing to smile no matter what, that was something Stacy had decided to try and never forget, knowing full well it could be something like that that might not surface until Patti was older.

"Let's see what's in the kitchen then!" Chad said, grinning even as he sensed a change in Stacy's body stance. Something was making her nervous. Was it something he should worry about, or was she just nervous about spending time with him in his home? After all, he was nervous about having her there, but certainly not for any wrong reason.

On entering the small open plan living area and kitchen, Stacy laughed. It was almost an identical replica of the little home that she and Patti lived in. She could see that discovery momentarily had confused Patti too.

"I know it's small…" Chad started to say, seeing the two of them look at each other with curious looks on their faces.

"It looks just like ours," Stacy said. "Honestly, it's almost *exactly* the same."

Chad was relieved. Nothing to worry about there after all.

CHAPTER 20

After the meal had been eaten, Stacy naturally moved toward the kitchen sink.

"I think not!" Chad said as he saw her start to fill the sink with hot water.

"I'm going to do the washing up," said Stacy.

"Stacy, you are my guest," said Chad. "If you want to help, you are very welcome to sit on the bar stool there and chat to me while I do this."

"Okay," said Stacy, automatically doing as he'd instructed her to do, until she considered she didn't want to get into that situation again – one where she was receiving and carrying out instructions as if she was a robot. "Actually, how about you wash and I dry?" she asked as she jumped up from the bar stool and walked around to where Chad stood.

Seeing her determination, Chad smiled at her and handed her a tea towel. If she felt she needed to do something to help him, and it was going to mean she was relaxed, he was more than happy to take that compromise.

"Deal," he said, loving the smile she gave him in that moment.

Going through the simple job of cleaning up the kitchen together, almost like two members of a team, Stacy found the experience odd but surprisingly enjoyable. She'd never gone through anything like it with her husband but, with Chad, it felt natural to be working together toward a mutual goal, and having a laugh in the process.

As the two of them finished up, she kept an eye on Patti, who was happily looking through one of her picture books.

"Let me know when you want to head off and I'll

give you a ride if you like," Chad said when the kitchen was tidy again.

"Oh, you probably need to do things…"

Hearing her uncertainty, Chad glanced at Patti, saw she was preoccupied, and seized the moment to move close to Stacy and give her a quick hug.

"I want you and Patti to stay as long as you feel comfortable to," he whispered in her ear. "Do you have time to come and chill on the sofa for a while?" he then asked as he held out his hand to her.

Experiencing yet another moment of uncertainty, Stacy placed her hand in his, just as Patti looked at them. Although there was no distress or anything other than happiness on Patti's face, Stacy naturally pulled her hand away as she followed Chad to the sofa. It felt nice when he held her hand, but how would Patti really be feeling about seeing her mother so close to a man other than her father? She was only a toddler. Wondering still worried Stacy.

As Chad sat down and relaxed back, he shifted his glance from Stacy to Patti and back again. With little Patti happily playing and reading in front of the sofa, Chad took a moment to think about the situation he might be embarking upon. He'd never before been involved with a woman who was already a mother, but he had always loved kids. Time was passing for the possibility of fatherhood to happen in his life, he'd often supposed, even though he certainly didn't feel old.

"You look thoughtful," he heard Stacy say quietly as she positioned her body so she could equally look at him and at her daughter.

"I sometimes wonder if I've left it too late to become a dad," Chad admitted.

"I think men can have kids at any age, right?" Stacy said, curious about where such a conversation could lead.

"Yeah, physically I guess," said Chad. "Sometimes

I still feel young. Other times, though, I feel very, *very* old."

"Well, you're hardly that! Do you feel that way because of your work?" asked Stacy.

"Possibly," Chad said. "Certainly some of the things I've seen have forced me to grow up a bit faster than what I might have done if I hadn't seen those things."

Stacy nodded. She wasn't exactly sure what his job entailed, other than escorting young women and their daughters to small towns, but she had heard him mention cold cases.

Thinking about that term – cold case – made a shiver run down her spine.

"Now, *you* look thoughtful," Chad said, seeing her face change.

"I don't want to ask about your work too much, but did you say the other day that you were here to work on a cold case?" Stacy asked and saw him nod. "*Murder* cold case?"

"Unfortunately," said Chad. "I can't talk about it too much while I'm investigating but, yes, I am working on a case that *probably* is one of murder, even though..." he started to explain before wondering if he really wanted to share any information in front of a woman who might have been through something horrid in recent times, and her young daughter.

"You don't have to explain anything more," Stacy said, not sure she could face hearing any more details. The word murder had crossed her mind many times over recent years, but not in relation to anyone other than herself. That was something she didn't need or want to disclose right at that moment. "But it must be a hard job to do."

"It is, but I always wanted to be in law enforcement, and it can be as rewarding as I thought it would be,"

Chad said. "Not always, but most of the time."

For a moment, he wanted to ask Stacy about any work she'd done. Instead he decided to let her share whatever she wanted to, and keep quiet with what she didn't.

"I feel blessed that I'm here," Stacy said, surprising him.

"Here, with me?" Chad asked, teasing her even though he knew she meant something entirely different. "In my living room?"

Stacy laughed softly. Yes, she was getting used to it always feeling so good to laugh, even if only a little.

"Exactly," she said as she grinned. "But you know what I mean, I'm sure! I feel blessed to be in Skagway, and I feel blessed to have been helped to come here. If that hadn't happened..." she started to say as horrific memories threatened to change the vibe of the evening.

"But it *has* happened, Stacy," Chad said as he moved a couple of inches closer and gently placed a hand on her shoulder. "No matter what you've been through, you *have* gotten away, and you *are* here, in this peaceful town, and you *are* here, in this little home with this absolutely gorgeous man."

Hearing his teasing, and his effort to relax her and make her laugh, Stacy giggled. She knew he wasn't being serious about the second half of his statement, but in that moment it most certainly *was* an absolutely gorgeous man that she saw beside her.

"I like spending time with you," she said as they smiled at each other. "I'd like to keep doing that whenever you return from whatever's taking you away."

Before he could reply, Chad saw Patti stand up and move to Stacy, silently asking to be picked up. As he watched mother and daughter settle into a well-practiced embrace, Chad grinned.

"I'll be back, don't you worry. And, when I am, I'll

be more than happy for you and Patti to come and have dinner here with me again," he said.

"Yay!" Patti said, making Chad and Stacy laugh while summing up exactly what they were both thinking.

"Yay, indeed, Little Miss," Stacy said as she pulled Patti closer. "Now, I think it is time that you and I left Chad, and we go home. Gather up your things into your bag and we'll get going."

Without hesitation, she saw Patti jump down off her knee and start putting things in her little backpack. While her daughter was busy, Stacy quickly leaned closer to Chad and placed her lips on his. It was over with almost as quickly as it had started, but it was enough to make her smile at the smile he was giving her in return.

"Right, let's get you both home," Chad said, feeling happier than he had in a while. What was it about the woman that held his attention so much? They'd only known each other a short time, and they'd hardly started to share details about each other's lives.

To his own question, he had no answer except that he *was* enjoying getting to know her, he *was* looking forward to seeing her again … and he *did* hope that it wouldn't be long at all before he was able to return to Skagway to hold and kiss her again.

CHAPTER 21

Monday morning brought a slightly busier time in the store than Stacy had experienced over her previous weeks of work. The 'slightly busier', she enjoyed and confidently handled, just as she did on the Tuesday, and then on the Wednesday. By Thursday, things were definitely getting busier still.

"You're doing well," Ella said to her when they had a quiet moment on the Thursday afternoon. "Honestly, if you hadn't said you had no experience working in retail, I'd think you'd been doing this for years. A natural!"

"Thank you, Ella," Stacy said. There was still nervousness around just how busy the store would get over the season, and how she could possibly handle that, but she was certainly relieved that customer numbers were ramping at a steady but slow rate. "I hope there are no regrets in employing me then?"

"None whatsoever," said Ella, laughing softly. "It'll get busier, but you'll be fine. It isn't easy, the cruise ship season, because it is seven days a week, but if you can handle the daily routine of things, you'll be fine."

Stacy took a moment to smile and simply appreciate where she was, and how different her life had become compared to months earlier. A part of her became angry when she thought about all the time she'd wasted, too afraid to get away from a situation that she'd known was bad. She had to keep replacing that anger with acceptance that it was what it was, and then joy at how her life was shaping up in the immediate moment.

"I forgot to ask – did that tall, dark and handsome detective find you last Friday?" Ella asked, surprising Stacy.

"Yep," Stacy replied.

"He seemed awful eager to see you," Ella said,

making Stacy chuckle at the suggestive tone in Ella's voice.

"And he found me," Stacy said.

"Don't give much away, do you," Ella said, grinning.

"Do you know him well?" asked Stacy.

"Nope! I haven't had any dealings with him, to be honest, but I have seen him around town a couple of times over the years," said Ella. "Seems nice enough, and he's helped out the sheriff before. If you want to get the low-down on him, Smithy's probably the best person to ask. She's known him for a while, I think, through work and socially."

"Yes, he said they'd met before he came here," said Stacy. "I like Smithy. Chatting to her doesn't feel like I'm talking to a deputy sheriff."

Hearing Ella laugh out loud made Stacy smile.

"Yeah, she's one of a kind, that one," Ella said cryptically, making Stacy wonder, not for the first time, what exactly the relationship was between the two women who'd proved so friendly toward Stacy already. "Now, do you want to run away and take a moment to yourself before you pick up little Patti? This late in the day, I don't expect we'll get busy now."

"Are you sure?" Stacy asked. "I don't mind working till closing…"

"I know, and I thank you but, honestly, the ships seem to be leaving a little earlier this week than they have previously, so passengers will be already on their way back to the ships. Go on and run along now. It's good to recharge when you can, for another busy morning tomorrow."

"But when do *you* recharge?" Stacy asked.

"Oh, this old girl doesn't need to," said Ella. "She's just plugged in all the time," she added before throwing her head back in laughter, as if she'd told the greatest joke.

"Okay," Stacy said as she giggled. "If you're sure…"

"Go! Like I always say, seize these quiet moments," Ella said, as if casting Stacy aside. "I'll see you in the morning."

After saying her goodbye, Stacy wandered along the street to the supermarket. Grocery shopping was another small chore that she'd missed out on for so long that now it felt like a joy.

"Are you missing him yet?" she heard Smithy's voice teasingly ask from behind her as she walked among the small aisles.

"I'm not sure who you're talking about, Deputy," Stacy teased back.

"Oh, I think you do," Smithy said as the two women came face to face.

"Smithy, you've known him for a while…" Stacy began to ask.

"Yeah, he can be a pain in the butt sometimes – like a big brother – but we get on well enough," said Smithy. "If you're asking me what he's like, Stacy, trust me - he's one of the good ones."

"That's a relief but…" Stacy again began to ask, not sure if she could find the courage to ask what she wanted to know.

"Come out with it! Just ask," said Smithy, her smile indicating she was almost daring Stacy to ask something she didn't want to.

"The two of you," Stacy said before seeing Smithy laugh out loud.

"Oh, Stacy, Chad and I met years ago, and have spent little snippets of time together over the years through work, but no, you have nothing to worry about there," Smithy said. "No, even if I liked boys (which I don't), no, he's a really good man, but he really is like a big brother. I can't imagine him in that way – not for me, I mean, but for *you*, on the other hand…"

When she stopped speaking, Stacy found herself momentarily speechless. There was a lot to process from the speech Smithy had just made.

"Oh, for me? What?" she finally asked when she'd played through the words in her mind.

"For you, dear Stacy," Smithy said as she linked her arm through Stacy's and they began to walk. "For you, Chad Andrews is a good man, and if you do reach a point where you want to give a good man a chance, I truly believe you'd be safe in his hands."

The words the deputy sheriff said confused Stacy. There could have been joy from the reassurance that Chad was a good man who wouldn't hurt a woman. There was also a reminder that not all men were like that, or what they seemed.

"Thanks," she said, not wanting to dwell on the men in the world that women most definitely were *not* safe around, even though all of those men had seemed nice at the start. "I don't know if anything will happen. He's not even in town…"

"Yes but only for now," Smithy said. "He told you he was only getting out of town to do something with his current investigation, right? He's coming back…"

"Yeah, but … he doesn't *live* here, does he," Stacy said, realizing she didn't actually know where he lived permanently.

"Ahh, now *that* is a very valid point!" said Smithy. "Look, his work takes him all over the place, sure, but I have a very strong feeling that *that* boy is moving towards wanting to settle down. Don't quote me on that – it's only a feeling I got in my gut – but I do think that if you're willing to give him a chance, it really could be good for both of you."

"It would get your seal of approval then?" Stacy

asked, smiling. "If something happened between us?"

Seeing the deputy nod and grin as widely as she did made Stacy happy. Surely the deputy sheriff would know if there was something off about Chad, and she would know what Stacy had been through with another man in another time. Stacy had to believe that Smithy wouldn't encourage such a friendship if there was anything to worry about. She *wouldn't!*

"Well, for now I am just happy to be in this town, and at the store with Ella…"

"Yeah, just watch out for that one," Smithy said as she started to walk away. "Get too close and she'll want to adopt you!"

As Stacy watched, she saw the deputy grin, wave, and then round the corner, leaving Stacy none the wiser about whatever it was between Ella and Smithy that made them talk about each other in such a teasing way.

Looking at her watch, she started to move more quickly. There was plenty of time to go and pick Patti up, and there was no reason to claim too much time in solitude, but what she found herself wanting most of all was to figure out a plan for the evening meal, and then go and give her daughter a great big hug.

CHAPTER 22

As Chad finished packing his overnight bag in preparation for leaving his current location and moving onto the next, he sat down on the bed he'd slept in each night since leaving Skagway.

Giving thought to the small town that he did have a fondness for, his mind naturally shifted back to Stacy. As busy as he'd been for the days since he'd left, she had continued to appear in his thoughts. Where he currently was, he'd spent time doing interviews with people who'd been interviewed about Missy's disappearance previously. As was the result of liaising with the locals in Skagway, nobody had much to add to whatever they'd said previously. It made things somewhat frustrating, and somewhat annoying, but he was committed to continuing until he could find the ultimate answer: what happened to Missy? What happened to her, and where was she?

The 'where' continued to be the biggest concern. Around Skagway were mountains of bush and trees, plus some areas of water. If anyone had hurt her, they'd unfortunately have had plenty of places to leave her. The remoteness of the area meant it was unlikely she would ever be found. That always made cold cases harder to solve. At least if there was a body, modern forensics might be able to figure something out from that. No body meant no forensic clues.

Picking up his notebook, Chad took some time to focus on what he'd planned was his next step in the investigation. He still had to jump on another plane to go and see more people who no longer lived in the Skagway area, before he could head back to Skagway, and back to where Stacy was.

He'd thought about her a lot since he'd left,

wondering if he should have asked for her number so he could call her, but what could he tell her if he did? He couldn't talk about things that people had told him. He couldn't talk about the case at all to her. How could that work in a relationship? He'd never figured that out at all, throughout his years in law enforcement. Again and again, it had been the reason he'd let relationship after relationship slip away, with whoever his partner had been at the time becoming fed up with him remaining closed up and not talking about the things he saw and heard each day.

Thinking back about the women he'd been involved with for varying periods of time, he could now hardly remember much about them. Some, he'd been physically attracted to, but there really hadn't been anything more to it than that. Those ones, he knew would never have lasted long, no matter what. Outer appearance was worth little in reality.

His ideal lifelong love – if there was one to be found for him – was going to have to be someone who he considered a best friend, more than anything. Someone he could confide in and share things with, without them wanting to jump in and provide their views on his activities or his life. Someone he could feel was an equal, who he could contribute 50% to a life together with, rather than everything being uneven and unequal.

"Ugh, stop!" he said out loud as he stood up from the bed. It was time to leave the hotel he was in, and leave the town he was in. That night he would be in another hotel, in another town, and sleeping in another bed. That was the way his life was these days, and it was a life he'd chosen to live and make so important. Perhaps the time might be approaching when he would want to settle down but, for the immediate moment, he had a job to do, and answers to find.

CHAPTER 23

Glancing down at where Patti played with the other children when Stacy picked her up from Ella's son's home that Sunday, Stacy felt calm. She hadn't known the family her daughter was spending weekend days with, but she saw nothing of concern when she took a spare moment to see how everyone in the large household was interacting with each other.

"She really is a joy to have here," Stacy heard Ella's daughter-in-law, Suzanne, say.

"I'm just so appreciative that you're willing to look after her on these days, Suzanne," said Stacy. "You don't know how much it means to me."

"It's no problem at all," Suzanne said, grinning. "To be honest, it's a relief for Zach to know his mother has some help at that store! For years he's been trying to tell her she needs to retire but she does love it so. At least he can rest easy now, knowing she isn't doing it all on her own, so don't worry about Patti coming here. You're helping us out by helping Ella, as much as we're helping you out!"

"Thank you," Stacy said. "I do love working with Ella. She makes me smile."

"Yeah, she's a laugh a minute," Stacy heard Ella's son, Zach, say as he walked past. His tone made it a little difficult to know if he was talking affectionately about his mother, or very sarcastically and not in a nice way. The uncertainty about the remark forced Stacy to smile but not say anything in response.

"Mommy!" Patti called out as she started to run toward Stacy. "Are we going home now?"

"We sure are!" Stacy replied as she bent down to deliver the silently-requested hug. "Grab your jacket and bag and let's get home so we can cook something yummy for dinner!"

As the two of them walked out of the door, Stacy felt an inkling of concern. Where it came from and what had inspired it, she wasn't sure, but concern was something that she knew well. Unfortunately, it was also something that she suspected she felt far too often – more often than it should have been needed. Knowing that, she filed it away as her simply being silly, and started to inspire her daughter to talk all about her day.

CHAPTER 24

"Hey, hey, you're back!" Chad heard when he walked into one of the local precincts he'd worked in before. The last time he'd been there had been the day he'd been told he was going to escort a woman and her daughter to Skagway. At the time, he'd thought nothing of it, and expected it would be something he'd do and then probably forget all about. In contrast, he could now remember that day very well indeed.

"Yeah, the case I'm working on has led me to interviewing some people here, so thought I'd call in," Chad replied.

"Boss is out right now but should be back in his office in a few mins," the officer said. "He'll be glad to see you."

Chad smiled and began to walk toward the police chief's office. He had no current business in the police station, but there was no harm in keeping up to date with anything going on. He'd done his last job there. He hoped all had gone well with that in the end, after he'd done what he'd needed to do.

"Hey Chad, what can I do for you?" he heard the Chief of Police ask as he walked into the office.

"I was just in town doing some work on the cold case I'm working on so thought I'd pop in and see how everything's going here," Chad said. "No problems with the case?"

"The mother and daughter who went to Skagway with you?" the chief asked, surprising Chad.

"No, the case I worked on with you before I went up there," he said.

"Oh, no!" the chief exclaimed. "That's all done and dusted, thanks to you. No, after a day of questioning, a confession came and a conviction was delivered. No problems at all there! But I am curious to hear how the Skagway deal went."

"What … what Skagway deal?" Chad asked. He didn't know if the chief was asking about the cold case he'd been assigned to work on in Skagway, or him escorting Stacy and her daughter to the small town. Either option surprised him as a topic of conversation.

"The mother and daughter!" the chief said, as if he thought Chad must be completely stupid for not knowing that. "They *are* still safe?"

"Yes," Chad replied, wondering if he was supposed to know something that he clearly didn't. "Both seem to be safe and sound, settled, and happy up there."

"Good to hear," the chief said. "Bad situation that one. Poor girl was terrorized by that bastard, but he's gonna get what's coming to him."

"Chief, I don't actually know anything about that situation," Chad said, sure he probably shouldn't be hearing whatever it was that the police chief seemed to be assuming Chad knew.

"Oh, no, of course you don't," the chief said, thoughtful. "Bad bastard, that one, but we have him under surveillance. Like I said, he's gonna get what's coming to him very soon. Rest assured of that."

"Right," said Chad, not really sure about anything the chief was saying. "Sounds like a difficult case that you guys might be working."

"Maybe," the chief replied. "Like I said, he's a bad bastard, with fingers in a lot of seriously messed up pies."

"Right," Chad again replied, growing more confused by the minute. "Well Stacy and Patti are doing great up there."

Seeing the chief look at him in surprise, Chad wondered if he'd said the wrong thing.

"It's a small town," he said when he realized he'd

probably sounded a little too familiar with the mother and daughter he'd helped move.

"Right," the chief said, smiling knowingly. "Be careful there, Chad. She's been through a lot."

"Oh, there's not…" Chad started to say. He caught himself and stopped speaking when he realized he might actually be about to tell a lie. Was there *not* something going on there, or *was* there something going on there? He knew he couldn't call it a relationship, but he probably shouldn't imply anything was definitely '*not*' when it came to him and Stacy.

"Just be careful," the chief said, as if to immediately shut that conversation down completely.

"Chief!" an officer suddenly said as he rushed into the office. "It's all go with Ricky Tennyson!"

"He's heading to the port?" the chief asked, obviously rattled.

"Nope, he's actually boarding the ship right now," the officer said.

Hearing the urgency in the voices of both men, Chad tuned into their conversation.

"Ricky Tennyson? That name sounds familiar. Who is that?" he dared to ask. The only reply he got was the two men looking at each other with uncertainty on their faces. "Chief, what's going on?"

"Nothing for you to worry about, Chad," the chief said. "I got this," he then said, dismissing the officer who'd walked into the office. "Now, while you're here, quickly fill me in on how that cold case of yours is going. Any luck moving forward with that?"

Although concerned about whatever was happening with someone obviously bad, and obviously on the move somewhere, Chad allowed the chief to change the subject. Whatever it was all about, it didn't appear he was supposed to know about it, and that was sometimes how things went in his job.

"I'm doing interviews with all of the people who were interviewed at the time," he said. "That's why I'm in town."

"Right," the chief said. The tone told Chad that the man facing him was distracted – distinctly so. "Well, I won't hold you up any longer then. Let me know if you need anything from us for the cold case."

Hearing the firm sound of dismissal in the chief's voice, Chad stood, shook the man's hand, and walked out. Something about that encounter had left him very uneasy, but he didn't know what questions to ask, or who he could ask them to. If he was meant to know anything, he assumed that in time he would.

CHAPTER 25

After completing interviews with all people he'd read about in the cold case files, Chad felt a blend of relief and frustration. He was relieved that everyone who'd been interviewed at the time, was still alive and had agreed to speak to Chad, albeit reluctantly in some cases. In contrast to that relief was the frustration that he didn't feel he was getting any closer to finding out what had happened to Missy. Nobody appeared to know anything, but he knew *somebody* must have known *something.*

On the final day away from Skagway, he took some time to lie down on the large hotel bed and think about the case investigation so far. He'd worked through every box that he'd been given in the small Skagway sheriff's office. From each box, he'd extracted the pages, one by one, and read everything, carefully making notes as he did. Had he missed something? What more could have been found out?

Thinking about the small township, and the location of what had been Missy's home, he took some time to visualize the area. She'd been seen leaving the small school that afternoon, but she hadn't been home when her mother and father had finished work. That was out of the ordinary, and the route from school to home was relatively short. Where did she go in-between those two locations? And, in such a small town where everyone knows everyone, how did nobody *see* whatever happened to her?

Casting his thoughts over the streets and the surrounding locations, he found his mind starting to drift along another path altogether. The waterfall. Having been up there twice with Stacy, now she was a part of the landscape as he imagined it. That wasn't good for the case, but it was certainly very enjoyable to cast his mind back and think about the times he'd spent sitting with her, and kissing her.

It wasn't what he should have been thinking about but, for a few minutes, he indulged in it. He didn't want or think it was fair to be in a relationship, and he wasn't a man who wanted to have one-night stands or short flings, but he couldn't deny his attraction to Stacy. Part of it was physical, but part of it was … what? Her intelligence? Her charm? Or was there something pulling him toward her out of some form of sympathy, knowing she must have been through something pretty bad if she'd been moved by law enforcement?

Knowing he could lie right where he was, simply indulging in remembering the sight, scent and sound of the woman he'd met so recently, he finally pushed himself to stand up. He'd finished what he had to do in that city. It was time to return to Skagway and figure it all out – the cold case *and* his feelings for Stacy.

CHAPTER 26

As Stacy embarked on another week of working with Ella, she felt her confidence growing. For far too long she'd let someone tell her she mustn't work – that it wasn't a woman's job to do that – but working in the small store felt so good!

Now and then she found herself thinking back to when she'd been a teenager, and how strong-willed she'd been during those years. That strong will had carried through to before she'd met Ricky, and even into the first few months when they'd started to date. But then … what had happened after that? Could she pinpoint the moment when he'd started to succeed in taking over control of everything she did? Had it started with just one little thing that she'd bowed down to him over and given him his way for?

Even as she tried to think back so she could answer those questions, she couldn't remember. The simple truth was that he'd started out charming, treating her like an equal and even pretending that he loved how independent she was. It had been a very subtle exercise for him to slowly but surely remove every shred of independence she'd once had.

"How are you going, Stacy?" she heard Ella ask from behind where she knelt, replenishing shelves.

"Yeah, I'm all good thanks, Ella," Stacy replied. She was already getting used to the increasing number of customers who were entering the store each day and needing assistance. It had taken her some time to get used to conversing with strangers again, but she was enjoying serving the diverse range of people who walked into the store. They were all on a dream holiday, and outwardly buzzing because of it. There was nothing serious or horrible in that. "Just about finished restocking these. They sure are popular!"

Hearing Ella laugh made Stacy grin. That was another thing that she was loving – smiling and laughing. Such simple things she'd stopped doing for so long, having had them beaten out of her – literally.

In the back of her mind, memories still flowed over her far too frequently, forcing her to think about her husband far too often. She wanted to be rid of the memories altogether. Instead she often found herself wondering where he was, and what he was thinking about her and his daughter having disappeared. Had he looked for them? Was he looking for them now? And if he wasn't – if she truly was safe from him – how would she ever know?

Also in the back of her mind was the ongoing expectation that at some point the police were going to come knocking on her door, giving her some form of ultimatum to help them put Ricky behind bars. Whatever he'd done, it must have been far more serious than just beating her. She'd still not been told anything about that side of things, and it was only a gut feeling that she was going to be needed for something, but that feeling hadn't left her since she'd boarded that first plane.

Remembering the plane rides that brought her to her current home, she smiled to herself. That was the day she'd first met Chad. She hadn't expected then that she would even see him again, let alone end up kissing him, but she loved thinking about him – and his kisses.

"Now *that's* a look I've seen many times before, but not on you," said Ella when she noticed the expression on Stacy's face. "Who is the cause of that, I wonder. Perhaps a tall, dark, handsome man in law enforcement?"

As Stacy stood and faced her boss, she giggled like she could remember having done when she was a kid.

"I'm not sure who you mean, Ella," she said, acting

coy.

"Uhuh," Ella said as the door opened and some new customers walked in. "Saved by the passengers."

Stacy grinned but got to work, serving customers while pushing Chad from her thoughts.

CHAPTER 27

Sitting on his final flight into Skagway, Chad's mind remained fully focused on his entire interaction with Stacy so far. The day he'd met her hadn't comprised exactly the same journey of flights as he was currently making, but the final flight was the same. When he'd looked at her that day, he'd seen a woman and a daughter who just needed to be escorted somewhere.

He'd assumed they'd needed to get away from their hometown for some reason, and that reason was probably serious, but he hadn't known any details then, and he still didn't. Was it something he should know before allowing himself to move forward into anything romantic with Stacy? He supposed the sheriff knew what her story was, and possibly Smithy too, but neither had warned him to stay away. Was that a good sign?

"Would you like tea or coffee, Sir?" he heard a flight attendant ask, surprising him since the flight was so short.

"No, thank you," he replied, knowing any kind of caffeine was the last thing he needed. For some, it stimulated the mind. For him, it only seemed to cloud it, always making him regret having had it.

For the remainder of the short flight, he relaxed back in his seat and looked out the window. Watching the white of the cloud and the blue of the sky, his mind shifted back and forth between the same two subjects that it too often did – what was happening with Stacy, and what had happened to Missy.

The duration of the flight brought no answer to either question at all.

CHAPTER 28

"Hey, you're back," Chad heard when he walked into the sheriff station on his arrival back in Skagway. "Any movement on the case?"

Turning around, Chad smiled. He hadn't needed to turn to see who was talking to him, but there was always something welcoming about seeing Smithy, with her eternally friendly nature and tone.

"Not yet, but it was still good getting to talk to everyone," he replied. "How are you going? Working hard?"

"Ha!" Smithy replied as she scoffed. "You know me too well to even ask that question but, yep, all is good with me … *and* I heard that a certain someone might have been missing you."

"I'm not sure who you could be talking about, Deputy," Chad said as the two of them fell in step together, walking toward the tiny office he'd been assigned for the duration of his stay in the small town.

"Hmm," said Smithy as she watched him plant his jacket and bag and immediately pick up one of the boxes from the corner of the room. "I thought you'd already been through all of those."

"Yep, but something is nagging me," Chad replied. "Have you ever heard of a guy named Ricky Tennyson?"

Hearing no immediate reply, he turned and looked at Smithy. The look on her face was one he'd never seen on her before – and he'd seen a *lot* of looks on her face over their time of knowing one another.

"You know something…" he said. "Smithy! What is it?"

"Maybe you better tell me why you're asking," Smithy said as she took a seat across from him.

"I just saw a chief I worked with on another case,"

said Chad, pushing the box aside and sitting down, leaning forward with certainty he was going to learn something that would make at least something fall into place. "He mentioned the name, and it seems familiar to me, but I can't pinpoint where I heard it."

"Well, did you *ask* him about it?" Smithy asked, seeming to try to appear like she was teasing him, despite her eyes showing an unusual level of seriousness.

"Yeah but he evaded my question," said Chad. "By the look on your face, I'm guessing *you* know something though."

"Maybe, but I don't know why you'd care about a guy from another state…"

Hearing the tone of her voice, Chad took some time to sit quietly as he studied her face. Smithy was one of the happiest law enforcement professionals he'd ever met, and hardly ever seemed serious, even when something serious was going down. For her to look like she did, Chad knew there was something about the name he'd asked about – Ricky Tennyson – that needed to be delved into far deeper.

Realizing he might have to figure out where he'd heard the name himself, he opened the box on his desk and started to pull out the pages. He was sure he'd looked at everything, but the name he'd heard hadn't been one that he'd put on a list to interview. Was it a name that he'd seen somewhere, associated with something to do with the cold case, or was he misassociating it altogether, and had heard it somewhere entirely different?

Knowing that could be the case, he began to act with speed, pulling out and reading pages one by one, letting his eyes skim over the words in the hope that either Ricky Tennyson would be a name he saw, or it wouldn't. Either result would be sufficient – at least he'd know one way or other if it was the current case or something entirely different he recognized the name from.

"I guess I'll leave you to it then," he heard Smithy say, making him realize only then that in the previous couple of minutes he'd entirely forgotten she was there at all.

"Yeah, thanks," he said as he took a moment to watch her walk out. He could have pressed her for more information, but her facial expression had clearly told him she wouldn't – or couldn't – tell him anything. Even so, the short interaction left him curious. What did she know about what he was asking about, and why was it such a big secret?

One thing he had worked out was that if he was going to figure out why that name had seemed familiar to him, he was going to have to find the reason himself. That meant going through every page in the boxes he had in his office, and studying every page again … and again … and again.

Most likely, in looking at Ricky Tennyson while still working on Missy's case, he'd find out that one thing had absolutely nothing to do with the other. If that happened, at least he could put his mind to rest about one of the lurking questions that kept plaguing his mind. That was better than where he was right at that moment.

CHAPTER 29

With every day that passed for Stacy, working in the small souvenir shop, she felt not only her confidence grow, but also her acceptance that her husband had brainwashed her into believing a woman should never work. If his beliefs were the truth, how could she love it so much, and, more importantly, how could her daughter be so happy when she finished each day at preschool if she hated being there too?

As faces came and went in the store, Stacy also found herself challenging any initial belief that Ricky had walked in. Her brain continued to play tricks on her, making her think this man or that man was him when the person first walked in. Taking a moment to force herself to actually look at the man and assess the truth seemed to be working. It was never him, and there was no longer any reason to be afraid. That discovery pushed her confidence up even higher – and her happiness.

"You look far more relaxed now than when you first started here," Ella said. It was one of several similar comments she made on a fairly regular basis, and they always made Stacy smile. "You're still happy to be working here?"

"Absolutely!" Stacy exclaimed. "I love working here! But you are right, Ella – I do feel better with each day, and I truly am loving this work. I think seeing the faces of such happy people is making things easy," she said before taking a moment to consider how unhappy she'd been for a long time. "To be honest, I've never seen so many happy people in my life."

Hearing Ella laugh instantly brought Stacy out of her own head and the thoughts that continued to plague her when they could.

"I'm sure you *have* seen as many happy people in

your life," Ella said as she continued to smile. "But I know what you mean. When we are in a place in life where things aren't going so good – when we have no reason to smile – it can seem as if we see no happiness anywhere anymore. But I believe everything that happens in life does happen for a reason. You are here, living happily in this new town and working in this little store of mine, and that has happened for a reason."

"I'm not sure what the reason for that could be," Stacy said, thoughtful.

"Maybe just because this is where you are meant to be," Ella reassured her as she patted her hand. "Accept that and life will become even happier. Now, this stock over here…"

Hearing Ella change the subject was welcome, as it always was. She had a way of making everything negative in Stacy's mind turn around and become positive. It was a trait that kept Stacy in awe of her boss – and the way fate had brought the two of them together.

Seeing Ella's face change from the seriousness of delivering instructions to one of a smile made Stacy curious enough to turn and follow her boss's line of sight. To her surprise, Stacy saw Chad enter and walk toward her. Feeling her heart instantly start to flutter was a strange feeling, but it was strong enough to hit her hard with the realization that she had moved beyond thinking about him as just a friend.

"Hey," Chad said quietly as he approached her. "Good morning," he added, facing Ella before she returned the greeting and then moved toward the rear of the store.

"Hi," Stacy managed to push out, feeling as if she was momentarily stunned from seeing him. There was no sound logic behind that but she didn't fight it. She liked him, and he was standing in front of her, giving her a grin that made her heart skip beats. What could possibly be wrong with that? "You're back."

"Yeah, I got back last night," said Chad. Glancing toward where Ella had moved, then at the doorway, he seized the opportunity to move even closer to Stacy and briefly put his arms around her. "I can't stop by for long, and I have to get back to work, but I wanted to at least say hi to let you know I'm here … and that I'm always thinking about you."

The statement surprised and stunned Stacy. What did it mean that he was always thinking about her? Her mind instantly wanted to hold onto those words and do an in-depth analysis on them. It took effort to dispel them from her thoughts and force her mind to go quiet again. The words were just nice words. There was no hidden meaning behind them.

"Me too," she said. It was the truth – she did think about him much more than she thought she should, so why not just be honest and admit it.

"I'll … I mean…" Chad started to splutter out. Why he couldn't suddenly string a sentence together, he had no idea, but he was sure it was ridiculous, to say the least. Not sure what he actually wanted to say, he quickly glanced at the doorway and Ella again before leaning down and gently placing his lips on Stacy's. It wasn't any kind of grand gesture, but it was certainly what he most wanted to do in that instant. "I have to get back to work but … can you be patient with me? My work…"

"Yes," said Stacy. "If there's one thing I am certain about with you and me, it's that we both understand the concept of patience."

Chad grinned at her. Of course she would be patient, just as he was committed to being patient with her. They both needed time and space, even if it was for completely different reasons.

After kissing her one more time, he walked out. There had been nothing arranged for them to see each other again – no activity and no date – but at least he'd seen her and made sure she understood that he certainly *wanted* to see her.

"I didn't see a thing," Stacy heard Ella say as she moved close.

Looking at the older woman's face, Stacy burst out giggling. Her boss didn't even try to hide the teasing expression that covered her face, or the cheeky grin.

"What was it that you said we needed to do now?" Stacy asked, laughing softly as she dismissed the conversation. The man she was enjoying getting to know had come into the store to see her and to make sure she didn't worry if she found out he was in town but not seeing her. He hadn't needed to do that, but it pleased Stacy that he had. It showed he'd been thinking about her in a very positive way, and that was something she'd been lacking for a very long time.

"How are you going?" Chad heard Sheriff Reed ask when his head appeared around the office door later that day.

"Yeah, good," said Chad. It wasn't entirely true – in truth he wasn't sure how much progress he was making on the cold case, but he certainly wasn't anywhere near giving up hope. There was something nagging him and that always meant there was something he was overlooking – something that might reveal an answer in the near future.

"Any new leads?" the sheriff asked, not moving from his spot in the doorway.

"There's certainly a lot to go over," Chad replied. "Some people have gut feelings about what might have happened to Missy, which is proving interesting."

Seeing the sheriff begin to laugh surprised Chad, but he forced a smile as he waited for the sheriff to explain what might be so funny.

"Don't take anything too seriously when it comes to gut feelings of the folk in this town," the sheriff said. "One thing I've learned over my long career in this job is that, especially here in Skagway, people talk, and sometimes words start spreading that aren't at all true. One person says something that's only their opinion but, then, before you know it, it's all over town and it's been blown *way* out of proportion. Stick to the facts, Boy, and dismiss everything else – that's where you'll find the path to success, I always say."

Chad smiled but didn't reply as he watched the sheriff retreat out of the doorway and then disappear from view. Chad had met people like that all of his life – people who only wanted to hear absolute facts – and he certainly respected that. Sometimes, though, it was the little things that people just thought, or assumed, or had an unfounded opinion on, that helped to solve a case.

Pushing the instance out of his mind, he grabbed a box and sat at the desk to go through the contents yet again. There was an answer somewhere. He just had to find it.

Picking up file after file, he hardly noticed the hours that passed. That was often the way. He had days when he was distracted but, when he let all daily aspects of daily life slip away and go quiet, he did have the ability to sit and absorb information for lengthy periods of time.

Glancing over a page in the late afternoon, he finally discovered where he'd read the name 'Ricky Tennyson' from. For a moment, he was dumbfounded. Passing his attention up and down over the page, he finally gained an understanding about why he'd had an inkling that things might cross over.

He was looking at a passenger manifest. It was long enough to almost be a book, with the number of passengers and the number of cruise ship crew that were in Skagway port on the day that Missy went missing. On that list was Ricky Tennyson, listed as a passenger, along with his wife, Monica.

Sitting back in his chair, he tried to figure out what the coincidence of that was, and why it was important. Ricky Tennyson was only one person on that list, out of thousands, so what was so special about him being on it?

With the question settling heavily on his mind, Chad stood up and started to pace. He'd heard the name in the town he'd worked another case on. It had been the chief of police who'd mentioned it – or one of his staff, when Chad had last been there. Ricky Tennyson. Chad had wanted to ask the chief what kind of case was forming around that person but the chief had blown the name off as if it centered around something Chad shouldn't know about.

Hearing Smithy's voice call out to another staff member as she entered the station, Chad jumped up to greet her and grab her attention.

"Hey, got a minute?" he asked. Seeing the smile on her face disappear told him that she could tell it wasn't a moment for the two of them to exchange their usual banter.

"What's up?" Smithy asked when she saw him enter her office behind her and then close the door.

"Ricky Tennyson," Chad said. "I know you know something, and you implied there's no reason for me to know about it, but ... there's some kind of connection here, Smithy – some connection between him and Missy's disappearance."

"What?" Smithy asked.

As Chad watched her expressions change, he only saw true surprise on her face. It confused him. He'd been sure that she knew something about the man in question, that might link him to the cold case.

"Why would you think that?" she went on to ask, sitting down.

Taking his time to sit down in the seat opposite her, Chad tried to figure out the connection in his head. Was there one, or was it just a coincidence? There were thousands of people on that manifest, after all. Any number of them could have been from the town that he'd previously been in.

"I don't..." Chad said, trying to find something in her voice or face that said she wasn't being truthful, but there was nothing like that for him to hear or to see. "Smithy, I get that you can't tell me about this guy but ... can you reassure me that he has nothing to do with Missy's disappearance?"

"Chad, I have no idea where you would get that idea from..."

"Because he's on the manifest of people who came

into Skagway that day!"

Watching the deputy further, he saw her surprise increase.

"Ricky Tennyson ... was in Skagway that day?" Smithy asked.

"Yes," Chad said. "Yes, he was on a ship, and he was here."

"I ... I think you need to leave that discovery with me," Smithy said cryptically as she stood.

"But..."

"No, just leave it with me, Chad!" he heard her say with enough passion in her voice to make Chad stop short of saying or asking anything more. He'd only ever seen Smithy be happy and laughing. At that moment, there was a level of seriousness on her face that he didn't identify with and couldn't comprehend.

Without any more words, he nodded at her, stood, and quietly walked out. They didn't know each other completely – as was evident by him not having seen her look like she did at that moment – but he couldn't let himself believe she was a law enforcement professional who would keep information to herself, especially when it might prove vital for a cold case – and a cold case centered around a young woman having gone missing at that.

Desperate to find out more, he returned to his office and sat down again. The manifest he put into a desk that held the pages he wanted to investigate again. Ricky Tennyson's name was on the list, and he was someone related to something that was going on in the city he'd recently been in. What was the case, and why was nobody able to share details of it?

CHAPTER 31

"Are you alright?" Stacy asked Chad when they sat up near the waterfall at the end of the week. She hadn't seen him since he'd walked into the store earlier in the week, telling her he was back in town, but she hadn't let herself think anything of it. He'd said his work was demanding of his time, and she was kind of relieved since it forced the two of them to go slow and not rush into anything bigger than either one of them could handle.

"I'm … yeah, sorry, work is … crazy," said Chad, regretful, as always, that he couldn't talk about anything specific to do with whatever case he was working.

"I know you can't share any information about it," said Stacy. "But how can I help with you feeling so … crazy."

Chad looked at her in surprise. It wasn't often that she said something so carefree and almost humorous. Seeing an attempted smile on her face made him grin.

"I'm always a little crazy," he said before reaching out and kissing her softly. "It is hard, being in this job. I just can't share much at all."

"But you need to," said Stacy. "It isn't the same thing but … I've been in a situation where things were happening and I couldn't tell anyone about anything. It … it's a horrible place to be, but I understand."

"Yeah," said Chad. "I think you do."

Reaching out and taking his hand in hers, Stacy smiled at him. There was nothing she could say or ask about whatever was plaguing him, and she did understand that predicament completely. She could also see exactly why a relationship might never work for him. That was a consideration that saddened her, but also relieved her. If he wasn't one to want too much from her, wasn't that a better scenario than someone wanting more than she could ever give?

"But enough about that," Chad said in an effort to change the subject. "How are you enjoying your work now that it's getting busier with all these ships coming in to town? Still loving it?"

"I am," Stacy replied. "Ella is wonderful, and so patient with me. She's taught me a lot, and I am enjoying seeing the passengers who come into town each day. I've never worked in retail, or in any kind of tourist place, so it's all new, but yeah, I do like it."

"I'm glad," said Chad before raising her hand to his lips. "You do seem happier each time I see you. It's good to see."

"Thank you," Stacy said.

Looking at his face and seeing the way he was looking at her, she felt a longing that she knew was growing and intensifying with each time she saw him. It was new for her – the natural desire and need to kiss someone – so there was an element of scariness in it, but also excitement.

Leaning in, she began to kiss him, softly at first and then more passionately as she felt her body react. It had been a long time since she'd felt awake in that way – truly awake and truly desiring of passion. She didn't want it to end – only to grow and intensify even more.

"Wow," Chad said when they broke apart. "You … you make it hard for me to walk away to go back to work," he added, laughing softly. "I'd much rather stay here and kiss you all afternoon."

"Me too, but I have to go and pick up Patti too," said Stacy, sad their time together was coming to an end again, but knowing it would always be best for her to take things slow if she entered another relationship. She'd rushed into the one she'd had with Ricky, and look where that had gotten her – not knowing who he truly was at all. "But I'm glad I ran into you and we got this time together."

"I'm sorry I can't make any promises about … *anything*, Stacy," Chad said, his tone changing from happy and giddy to serious. "I wish I could."

"I know," said Stacy as they stood. "Can we just enjoy this for … this? I don't want … I don't *need* to rush into anything … big. I would like you and I to … I just don't know where my own head is at."

As Chad listened to her get her words out, he could tell she was as flustered about their situation as he was. It was like they were meant to be together, but the universe wasn't quite sure that was the case at all.

"I am very happy for us to not rush, and to enjoy this … for this," he said, smiling as he mirrored what she'd just said.

When he saw her move closer to him, wrap her arms around his waist, and lean up to kiss him passionately again, he happily obliged. His body wanted more – so much more – but he was happy she'd said she didn't want to rush into anything. If there was a future to be had, they were building a solid foundation. That was more important than anything else – even if her kisses were starting to drive him a little crazy.

"I think we need to get out of here," he said, teasing her as he pulled away.

Seeing the smile on her face was a perfect thing to see before he returned to the seriousness of a cold case.

CHAPTER 32

As Stacy held Patti close to her that night, watching the flames glowing in the small fireplace in their living room, she cast her mind back to the short time she'd spent with Chad that day. When they'd kissed, she'd felt her body grow alert in longing. It had been such a long time since she'd felt that, that it had surprised her. If anyone had asked her about the feeling of passion, she might have told them that feeling had died inside of her, and her body no longer wanted anything to do with it. How wrong she would have been if she'd said that.

Sensing Patti wanting to get down from her lap, she focused on the routine they had of Patti using the bathroom, getting into her own bed, and the two of them taking some time to smile at one another before Stacy would see Patti's eyes begin to close.

Once sure her daughter was sound asleep, Stacy quietly walked back into the living area and resumed her stare at the flames as her mind drifted again.

Thinking about the kisses, she lifted one finger and gently ran it over her lips. When Chad had kissed her – and she had kissed him – their lips had danced happily together and it had all felt very natural. Over their time of knowing each other, since their first little kiss, passion had started to edge into their kissing, and their kissing sessions had started to increase in intensity and length.

The longer she sat, watching the flames flickering while thinking about the last kiss she'd shared with him, the more alert she grew to the fact that one part of her was beginning to throb. It had been so long since she'd felt it that she almost missed it was happening.

After getting up and quietly tiptoeing to Patti's room to double check she was still fast asleep, Stacy sat again on the sofa and lowered her hand to between her thighs. She wouldn't do anything there, but, for the first time in years, she took time to touch herself. Clothing separated her hand from where it wanted to touch, but she didn't rush to change that. Feeling and remembering the gloriousness of a soft caress over her entire crotch through her clothing was as much as she could handle for the moment. Anything more, she might work towards facing another day – perhaps when she was fully healed from the memories of having been touched with nothing but harsh pain in recent years – but, for that moment, it was more than enough.

A long while later, as the flames dimmed, she smiled to herself. She'd lightly touched herself with kindness. It was too long since that had happened. She would try it again another day, but now it was time to sleep.

CHAPTER 33

"Where are you heading off to in such a hurry?" Chad heard Smithy ask as they passed each other in the station corridor a week later.

"Heading out of town for a few days," Chad called back, not stopping to explain anything.

For days, he'd been going through all of the pages of the boxes in his office, over and over again. He'd found no more mention of the name Ricky Tennyson on any other page, and when he'd tried to log into the law enforcement database to search for information about Tennyson, Chad had come up against a brick wall. Whatever was happening about that man in the other city, it was locked off to whoever wasn't working the case. That was often how things went, Chad knew, but somehow he *had* to get some answers because coincidences rarely turned out to be just that.

"Okay," he heard Smithy call back. Usually their interactions were easy going. Since he'd started to try and get more information out of her, things had cooled slightly between them. It wouldn't always be the same, he knew – they'd had moments of awkwardness before when one of them had needed information and the other hadn't been in a position to be able to provide it. They sometimes had those moments, but they always got through them, and they would this time too.

Glancing at his watch, he saw he had enough time to call into Ella's shop and briefly see Stacy. They hadn't seen very much of each other at all over the previous few days, and there was frustration in the way they had to keep stealing moments now and then, without any certainty about when they might next be able to steal another. He couldn't deny, however, that she'd been incredibly understanding about his inability to make any promises to her. He also couldn't deny how amazing it felt every time he saw her – not to mention just how incredible it felt to hold her and kiss her. There was no lack of passion between them, but he was glad they weren't rushing there either. He'd had relationships fuelled by physical attraction in the past. They never lasted, and there was sadness in that, but he knew his connection to Stacy was far beyond the physical, even if he had found himself longing to be close to her.

"Hey," he heard Stacy call out as he entered the store. In the far corner he could see Ella serving a customer. Glancing around, he was relieved to see no other customers in sight. "What's up?"

Remembering how she'd reacted to his grabbing her arm when they'd gone for a walk weeks earlier, Chad gently placed his hand on hers and guided her behind a tall row of shelving. He'd meant to just walk in and tell her he was leaving town for a few days. When he looked at the concern in her eyes, and the lusciousness of her lips, he couldn't stop himself from indulging in kissing her.

As their lips moved together, Stacy had to force herself to not indulge too much. It felt glorious, but she was in her workplace. With regret, she pulled away.

"Wowza," she said quietly as she smiled at him. "Perhaps you better tell me what's going on."

Chad grinned ruefully, not entirely sure what had just come over him. He was acting like a teenager who was embarking on the newfound joy of physical touch.

"Sorry…"

"Absolutely no need to apologize for that," said Stacy, giggling quietly. "But what is up?"

"I'm just about to leave town – not for long, hopefully, but definitely for a couple of days at least," Chad said.

"Okay," Stacy said. Inside, she felt a deep change in

her happiness, but she also knew he was doing something amazing and something very, very important. "Well, I'll see you when you return, right?"

"Definitely," said Chad before leaning in and kissing her lips gently. "I'll come and see you when I get back?"

"Yes please," said Stacy before watching him deliver her one more smile and then was gone.

As Ella finished serving the customer, she approached Stacy.

"Is everything okay?"

"Yes, he just called in to say he's got to leave town again," said Stacy.

"You two certainly make a good looking couple," she heard Ella say, making her smile.

"Yeah?"

"Yep, and believe me, in my long life, I've seen a *lot* of couples who *weren't* good looking!" Ella said, making Stacy laugh out loud at the obvious attempt to shock.

"You are certainly one of a kind, Ella," Stacy said, grinning as she gave the older woman a quick hug. "And you are greatly appreciated."

"Oh, enough of all this soppiness! Come on! Back to work!"

As Stacy laughed in reply, she felt happy. Yes, the man she was enjoying getting to know was leaving town again, but she still felt happy. Was that normal? Inside she knew it wasn't only normal, but it was right. She'd been emotionally held captive by someone in her past, and now she was with someone who let her be free, and let her be herself. That was more than enough reason to be nothing *but* happy.

CHAPTER 34

As Chad made his way from his destination airport to the police precinct, he continued to try and formulate some kind of reason behind his thinking. Was there any connection at all between one name that had been on a cruise ship manifest from that particular day, and also mentioned in passing at a police station in another state? Logic argued inside of his mind, stating that of course it could be a coincidence, while also stating that there was no such thing as coincidence.

By the time he reached the police station, he was fired up and full of questions. He knew there was the strongest chance that he wouldn't get any answers to those questions, but he equally knew he had to try.

Without asking anything of anyone, he strolled through the police precinct and straight into the office of the police chief.

"Chad…" he heard the man behind the desk start to ask in surprise.

"Ricky Tennyson," Chad said, as if context was completely not required to get the answers he needed to get.

"How about you…" the police chief started to say as he pointed to the chair facing him.

"I know I'm not on the case but…"

"Sit down, Chad," he heard the police chief say with an increasingly less friendly tone in his voice. "What's all this about?"

"I need to know…"

"Why?" the chief asked.

"I think there's some kind of link between him and the cold case I'm working on in Skagway," Chad said, trying to keep his cool even though he felt adrenalin flowing through his body.

"You think… why would you think that?" the chief asked, leaning forward as if he was expecting to learn something he didn't already know.

"His name is on the manifest of a ship that called into port that day – the day that Missy Jameson disappeared," said Chad. "I know it's a long shot but … I just think there's some kind of connection here. What … *what* is the story with this guy?"

For a long while, he watched as the chief relaxed back in his seat again and then sat silent, studying Chad's face.

"You think … there's some chance that … Ricky Tennyson was a passenger on a ship that stopped at Skagway…"

"I don't just think that," Chad said. "He was!"

"And that he got off that ship while it was in port, and … did … something … to your victim," said the chief, his words portraying a question even though the tone didn't match.

"I do," said Chad.

"Hmm," the chief said.

Once again, Chad sat quietly as he watched the chief appear to consider the possibility. The fact that the idea hadn't immediately been shut down made Chad wonder if his suspicion might, in fact, be right – and might be something the chief had already considered.

"Well?" Chad asked. He wasn't usually one to ask too much of people in such positions, and he usually took pride in using the best possible manners, but he needed to find something to help with the case he was working on, and he definitely was losing patience with what others might call a coincidence.

"I think I need to process this a bit further," said the chief. "What exactly is recorded about this person up there – in Skagway?"

"Just that he was on the ship that day," said Chad.

"Nothing else?"

"I've been through every page of every file I've been given, and I've spoken to every person who was in the town at that time…"

"Except ship passengers and crew," the chief said.

"Right," Chad confirmed. "My initial thinking was that someone off a ship could have done something to Missy but…"

"But?"

"But the ships are only there for maybe eight hours or so, and if someone came off a ship and did something to a local person, what could they then do with the body?" Chad asked, knowing that was the biggest flaw with his theory, even though he kept feeling like he had to overlook that issue.

"That's true," said the chief. "And yet, here you are, thinking that someone that *we* are currently keeping an eye on, has something to do with that cold case *you're* working on."

"Yes," said Chad. "I know it sounds farfetched but … I just don't like coincidences, Chief."

"And that, I do understand," the chief replied, nodding. "But like you said, let's say Ricky Tennyson was on a ship that day, and he did somehow come across your victim, and he did do something to her … then, what? He got back on the ship and cruised away? That's not much time to do something like that and then get rid of the body. The body's never been found, right?"

"Correct," Chad said. "Yeah, I know that's … that's what makes this theory not … solid."

"You're right," said the chief. "It doesn't make a solid possibility at all. However…"

On hearing the chief's tone change, Chad felt his heartbeat speed up. He'd expected to be told he was being stupid – that there was no possible way it was Ricky Tennyson who'd done something to Missy and then gotten away with it – and yet the possibility didn't seem to be completely ruled out either.

"He is known to have a thing for young women," the chief said.

"How young?" Chad asked, sitting forward in anticipation, sure that he had to learn *something*.

"Teenagers," said the chief. "That is what we're building a case against him for."

As Chad listened and processed the answer he'd been trying to seek for what seemed like far too long, he hoped the chief would continue to provide more details. He didn't.

"So he *is* someone who could have done something to Missy," said Chad and saw the chief nod.

"Given his usual behaviors, it is possible, yes," the chief confirmed.

"Well, is he in custody for whatever you think he's done?" asked Chad.

"No, we're monitoring him until we can find something solid to use against him," said the chief.

Chad nodded, understanding fully how long it could take for law enforcement to have enough to get a solid conviction against someone, no matter how bad their crimes.

"Well, is there any reason I can't find him and talk to him?"

That answer, he got no reply to for a painfully long time. For the duration of the silence that ensued, Chad could see the chief weighing up options before he would give Chad an answer to that question.

"We know that right now, he's not in town," the chief finally said, his face revealing an extreme level of seriousness.

"Sure, but you know where he is. Where is he?" asked Chad, experiencing a sudden feeling of dread flowing over him.

"He's on a ship…"

"Where?"

Without hearing an answer, Chad considered what he guessed was probably going to end up being true.

"Tell me he's not on a cruise…" he said and saw the chief nod, his face looking increasingly grim by the minute. "To Alaska."

"Yes."

"To Skagway," Chad surmised.

"Yes."

Chad took some time to think about what he'd learned. The man he thought might have something to do with a young woman's disappearance years earlier might be about to visit the same place again. If he was responsible for Missy's disappearance, might he try and do a similar thing again?

"When's he due to dock there?" he asked.

"Tomorrow morning," said the chief. "But…"

Chad waited as he tried to analyze a plan. What did he hope he could achieve, even if he returned to Skagway? What could he do, even if he found Ricky Tennyson there and could confront him?

"We're building a case against him, Chad," said the chief. "If you go at him like a bull in a China shop, you could ruin everything we've been building. Please don't do it."

The options before Chad felt immense. He knew all about how a case could be compromised and even thrown out completely if things weren't done right. If this guy was an abuser – and a killer – Chad wouldn't be able to live with himself if he did anything that could interfere with Tennyson being put away, even if that did mean not learning what had happened to Missy.

"Right," he said, not sure what to do. "I … what do you recommend?" he asked, very prepared to listen to the police chief's recommendation about how things should be handled.

"I have no idea if he is responsible for the young woman you're trying to get answers for," the chief said. "What I do know is that this guy, we have to get off the street, and soon. The destruction he's leaving…"

"Well, what if there's a chance that he did do something to Missy Jameson in Skagway, and the fact that he's gotten away with it makes it the perfect place for him to return to and do the same thing again to some other young girl?" Chad asked. "How can we just let him go there and do that if we think it is a possibility?"

The chief took more time to consider options. Eventually, he leaned forward and spoke again.

"Maybe it is time," the chief said. "Maybe the time's come for us to bring him in."

"What?" Chad asked, his confusion never seeming to end.

"Yeah, I can't live with another young woman having done to them what we believe he's done to others," the chief replied. "Give me a minute."

Chad sat still as he watched the chief walk out of the office. In the silence that hung around him for the next ten minutes, Chad had time to think about possible ways to handle all of the news he'd gained. The man who could be responsible for Missy's death might be on his way to Skagway – the very place he might have done something to Missy. If that was the case, he could be planning to do the same thing again to another young woman. How could they stop him from doing that? If they pulled him aside in Skagway to question and accuse him, what could that do to the case already being built against him?

"Chad, this is Pete and Gordon," the chief said as he walked back into the office with two men behind him. "They'll accompany you part of the way tonight and then back to Skagway first thing in the morning to apprehend Tennyson when the ship arrives."

Still in a slight state of confusion about all that was happening, and the speed it was happening, Chad stood and shook each man's hand. It was a lot, and not in line with anything Chad had considered as a viable plan of action, but he knew better than to interfere with an ongoing police investigation. They were the ones who'd been following and monitoring the suspect, and they should be the ones to pull him in for questioning.

"We understand our case might overlap with your cold one," Pete said to Chad. "We can fill you in with all that we know about this guy on the way to Skagway."

"Okay," Chad said, eager to get going.

When the three men were walking out, Chad heard the chief call him back.

"Chad, wait! Shut the door for a minute."

Wondering what was coming, Chad did as instructed and then turned to face the chief.

"I think there's something important that you should know," the chief said, his face grave. "That woman – the woman you helped move to Skagway with her young daughter…"

"Yeah," Chad said, feeling dread begin to flow over him. "What about them?"

"They … she … she's his wife," the chief finally said.

Even though the words sounded clear, Chad was momentarily stunned into confusion.

"What?" he asked for clarification.

"The woman that you escorted to Skagway – she is … the wife … of Ricky Tennyson," the chief said. "The little girl – she's his daughter."

On hearing the situation explained so clearly, Chad had to sit down again.

"You sent her to … did you *know* he was planning to go to Skagway on this cruise, when you sent her there?" Chad asked in disbelief. He desperately wanted the answer to be no. He also knew that people didn't tend to get on cruise ships at the last minute before they set sail. "Chief, that wasn't that long ago. Did this guy already *have tickets* to go there when you asked me to escort her and her daughter to Skagway?"

Seeing the chief nod, Chad felt an emotion flow over him that he hadn't experienced for a long time – anger.

"So … you had been watching this guy for all of this time, and you *knew* he was going to be going on a cruise, so you helped his wife and daughter escape … to the very place you *knew* he was going to visit on the ship?"

"She's …" the chief started to say, his face betraying how uncertain he was that his plan was a good one at all.

"Bait," Chad said in realization. "You have sent a traumatized woman to a small town, and let her believe she's been able to begin to set up a new life – a safe life, away from a man who has abused her – when all along you've sent her right into the *path* of that man? What is *wrong* with you?"

Knowing he shouldn't have been speaking like he was to the Chief of Police, Chad didn't stop in his words of anger and disbelief. He'd heard of police using people as bait, and he'd heard of all sorts of crazy carry-ons to try and catch criminals, but what he was currently hearing, he could hardly believe.

At first, he felt indignant that everything he'd heard must be regarded as the complete wrong way to carry out a case. Then his mind – and heart – shifted to an entirely different consideration.

"Stacy," he said to himself as he comprehended the danger she was about to be put in. "You're putting her in danger!"

After a moment of silence, the chief nodded.

"For good reason," he said quietly.

Not believing what he was hearing, Chad knew he couldn't listen to any more. Standing, without further delay, he rushed from the office to find the other two officers, gather up their travel details, and prepare to rush to the airport. It was bad enough, all that he'd heard. Thinking about Stacy being put in danger by the possibility of the man she'd worked hard to try and move on from, finding her, was more than Chad could bear. He had to get back to Skagway and somehow get her to safety.

He *had* to!

CHAPTER 35

Throughout the long journey back to the sleepy little town, Chad conducted his own in-depth investigation into Ricky Tennyson via the two officers traveling with him. They knew what they could tell him and what they couldn't, and he knew he wouldn't learn everything there was to know about the criminal, but he was sure going to try and learn as much as he could, while he could.

In the morning, as soon as he boarded the final plane that would take him back to Skagway, he felt his heartbeat increase dramatically. Adrenaline continued to flow through his body, making him fully aware of how little sleep he'd gotten the night before. Over and over he'd replayed the entire conversation with the police chief. No matter what angle he looked at it all from, nothing made sense to him. All he could do was put faith in the possibility that there was a good reason everything had been done the way it had, and some kind of good outcome lay ahead.

Within hours, the criminal would be back in the small town, and he would be there for quite a few hours.

Hours. Was such a small amount of time long enough to do something to someone, and then hide their body so well that they would never be found? It seemed so little time to do something so big, but he knew that history held a great many stories of people who'd met their fate with such swiftness. And Skagway, although small in the centre of town, was huge when it came to mountainsides of trees and bush.

Despite his increasing belief that Ricky Tennyson was the one who must have done something to Missy — and the hope that he might be able to reveal where Missy was — Chad found his eagerness to get to Skagway wasn't due to that case at all. No, his eagerness lay fully with that one other snippet of information he'd gained – that Stacy was, in fact, Tennyson's wife.

How did Chad feel about that? He'd learned she was married, of course – she'd been open about that once they'd started to really get to know one another. And although she had never said what she'd been through, Chad had held suspicion all along that she'd been put through something horrific. That was why he'd thought she'd been moved with the help of law enforcement in the first place. Of course, now he had to question that as well.

The chief had implied she'd been moved not for any reason to do with her own safety, but for the convenience of law enforcement, as some kind of bait that might prove helpful when Ricky Tennyson saw her.

How did that make sense though? Chad wasn't sure what the ultimate plan was, but it seemed more than a bit stupid, not to mention needless. Stacy had been living with her husband, so could have been used at any time by police to get to Tennyson in their hometown. What was it about her and Tennyson that had inspired the plan that seemed to currently be in place? That he would see her in a remote Alaskan town when he was on a cruise? How could that be for certain either? Sure, Skagway was small, but he'd have to pick that one store out of the many that were in the town.

Nothing made any sense, as far as Chad was concerned. All he could do was help the officers to locate and apprehend Tennyson, and try to ensure Stacy and little Patti were kept safe.

As soon as the plane landed, he told the officers he would escort them to see Skagway's sheriff and then leave them. There was somewhere important he needed to be.

Somewhere far more important.

CHAPTER 36

Having arrived at the store nice and early, just as she tried to do every morning, Stacy once again relished the simplicity of sitting in the sunshine, on that old wooden seat, breathing in the fresh air. It had become a daily ritual that she never tired of. Around her was crisp, fresh air, and the beauty of nature. She'd ignored such things for most of her life. Now she absolutely loved it all.

"And there she is, reliable as always," she heard Ella's voice call out when she neared. "Ready for another busy day?"

"Sure am!" said Stacy, recognizing a fairly new enthusiasm that still felt invigorating to her.

Moving into the store, both women got to work, doing their first chores of the day as if they'd been working together for years. Every time Stacy considered that going to work and serving customers felt like a very normal thing she was doing, she smiled to herself. There was nothing to feel bad about, like she'd had programmed into her. Nothing at all.

"Oh, wow, that's gonna make things interesting today," she heard Ella say with a surprised tone in her voice.

"What's…" Stacy started to ask before she looked toward where Ella was standing, and saw raindrops hitting the window. "Huh! I'd forgotten all about rain. Isn't that ridiculous!"

Seeing Ella turn and look at her with surprise, Stacy grinned ruefully. The statement had been true – but she hadn't needed to say it.

"I suppose it is the first time you've seen it rain since you arrived," said Ella. "This place certainly isn't a desert but we haven't had anything like this for a few months."

"People must need it though, don't they?" asked Stacy as both women stood close to the window, observing the rain slowly but surely starting to get heavier.

"It is very much needed," Ella said. "For some, it'll be very welcome. Probably not for the tourists coming into town today though!" she added with a slight laugh in her voice.

"Will we be busier than normal then?"

"Maybe, but maybe not," said Ella. "Some who may have planned to get off the ship and walk around, might decide to stay on board instead if it doesn't clear. Others won't be bothered by a few raindrops, I'm sure, especially since it's the only day they get to see the town. One thing I've noticed over all of my years of watching those ships come and go is that there's no real pattern to the number of passengers who come and walk through the town. All we can do is be prepared and smile a lot after a good, busy day."

As Stacy watched her boss, she saw her give a reassuring grin and then turn, dismissing the rain as the working day began.

When the first few passengers of the day started to trickle in, Stacy relished the opportunities to talk to new people. Everyone she got to interact with seemed to be very friendly and polite. She knew not everyone was like that in the world, and she suspected not everyone was like that even on the confined space of the cruise ship, but nobody who'd entered the little store since she'd started work had been anything but nice. For that, she was glad.

CHAPTER 37

"Where do you think you're going?" Sheriff Reed asked Chad when he'd introduced the two officers and had then tried to make a quick getaway.

"I … I have to be somewhere," said Chad. When he was honest with himself, he knew he was frazzled in a way that wasn't normal for him. It probably should have been due to the knowledge that a man was coming to town who was suspected of having an unhealthy obsession with teenage girls, and had also been in town when Missy had gone missing. Instead, he knew it was due to the possibility that Stacy was going to be within dangerous distance of the husband who'd treated her so badly.

"I know where you're going," said the sheriff as he stood and walked up to Chad. "She isn't your priority today."

"Well, she should be," Chad replied. "Isn't she the very reason this guy's been allowed to leave his hometown? Because he *is* coming here, where she was placed by law enforcement, in the hope that … what, exactly? I still don't understand why or how any of this has happened."

"I know you don't, and you don't need to," the sheriff said.

"She is a mother … to a young daughter!" Chad called out with passion as the full weight of how much he'd come to love spending time with Stacy and Patti hit him. "And they are in danger! What kind of plan is this anyway? It doesn't make any sense!"

For minutes that followed, silence ensued. Behind the sheriff, Chad could see the officers glancing at each other, as if they, too, knew something that Chad didn't. It was frustrating and, in his opinion, it wasn't right, whatever it was that they had planned.

As the silence continued, with the sheriff and Chad looking at each other, deep in thought, Chad wished he'd asked Stacy for a number to contact her on. She'd told him she had a simple no-frills phone that she'd been issued with by law enforcement, but she didn't really need to use it so it spent more time in a drawer than on her. When she'd talked about it, he'd laughed with her and agreed that a phone was hardly needed in a town so small that everyone could just walk to see each other. Now he wished more than anything that he'd gotten that number. If he had that, he could have called her ahead of even getting back to Skagway, and warned her…

"This has to play out," the sheriff said cryptically. "You can't warn her."

Unlike his usual self, Chad was in disbelief. The only thing he could do to make himself feel relaxed again was tell himself that sometimes law enforcement did weird things for the right reasons. If he focused on that – that there was a good reason for everything that was happening – all would play out and all would be well.

Despite his gut telling him to run to that store and stand guard over the woman he knew was meant to be in his life, Chad Andrews finally sat down and started to listen to all that was about to be discussed about Ricky Tennyson, about Tennyson's wife Stacy, and about all that would be achieved before that cruise ship left Skagway at the end of the day.

CHAPTER 38

The first hour of the morning was quiet in the small souvenir store, even after the one ship coming into port that day had arrived. Following that first influx of customers walking in and happily buying their trinkets, a time of no activity followed.

"I might use this time to go out back and grab some more stock," Ella said to Stacy.

"Yep, I'll get this lot tidied up," Stacy said, grinning as she noticed yet again how much her neatly lined shelves seemed to never be anywhere near as neat when customers had been and gone.

She was happily moving this souvenir and that when she heard the door open, and the door close. Turning to face whoever had walked in, she froze.

On first sight of him, she tried to do as she'd been doing – tell her brain over and over that it wasn't him, it wasn't him … it wasn't him…

Except this time … it was.

Glancing around to see if Ella was in sight and might be able to deal with any conversation, Stacy instantly regretted having found the confidence to deal with customers alone.

In the seconds that followed, time seemed to pass incredibly slowly, providing enough opportunity for Stacy to assess what was before her.

Ricky was there – this time, it was no trick of her mind – and he wasn't alone. Beside him was a woman Stacy had never seen before. As Stacy's alertness grew, her focus fell on the way that Ricky's hand was gripping the woman's forearm. That was a move that Stacy knew well. To others, it was meant to look like a move of intimacy and care. In truth, it was a move of force, used to hold the woman in place, right where Ricky wanted her, and to use his fingers to dig into the arm if ever the woman tried to move away or even look unhappy to be right where she was.

Yes, Stacy knew that move well, and it made her curious about the woman. Stacy hadn't left her previous home very long ago but Ricky was standing right there, in front of her, with another woman. Was he on a cruise, on that ship that had just pulled in? Or had he located her so easily that he'd just come to Skagway to find her? But then, if that was the case, why did he have another woman with him?

Shock transformed into curiosity and then confusion. Why was he there, in the town Stacy had set up a new life in, and why was he there, in the very store that Stacy worked in? Coincidence? She couldn't know for sure but she supposed she would soon find out.

As she stood watching the couple move from shelf to shelf, she began to analyze their movements. Over her time with Ricky, she'd gotten to read his body well and, at that moment, it told her he hadn't yet seen her. Perhaps he was in the town to find her but, if he was, he didn't seem to be looking around to see if she was nearby.

Aware that an opportunity might have presented itself when she could move out the back of the store and ask Ella to swap places and tasks, Stacy started walking backwards. As she held her focus a little too much on the couple, she stumbled into a freestanding shelf designed for postcards.

That was the moment that Ricky Tennyson – husband, and wife beater – turned around and saw the wife he hadn't given permission to leave.

Before Stacy could do anything more, he was on her. As had happened far too many times before, her husband moved with speed to grab both of her arms, shake her, and then slap her sharply across the face.

"What…" Stacy heard Ella start to ask from a distance, just before Stacy felt Ricky throw her to the ground and sink the hardest boot into her gut that she'd ever felt in her life.

"You think you have the right to leave me, you…" Stacy heard Ricky call out to her, embarking on a long string of expletives he'd never shied away from using. "You're worth nothing to me. *Nothing*!"

As Stacy watched, she saw the woman who'd been by Ricky's side look at her with tears in her eyes, slowly shake her head and mouth 'sorry', and then run out the door. Stacy's only thought about all of that was 'yes, that's the right thing to do - run while you can.'

More kicks to her gut. More punches on her head.

Then there was only blackness.

CHAPTER 39

After far too much chatter in the office of the sheriff, finally Chad was released. It was absurd, to say the least, how the sheriff had insisted he, the two officers and Smithy had remained within those four walls, listening to talk, talk, talk, while knowing a dangerous man was in the township, wandering around. And for what? Some plan that didn't even make sense?

"She's gonna be okay, Chad," Smithy said to him even though her voice betrayed a level of concern he hadn't seen on her before. "Come on, let's go get him."

Jumping into her car, Chad felt dread flow over him. Maybe they were all overreacting. Maybe the guy had gone on an excursion that would fill in the whole day, and had no desire to even see the town. Hell, maybe the guy wouldn't even get off the ship, given just how miserable the weather had turned out to be.

"This rain is crazy," he heard Smithy say, as if to distract him from his increasing concern for Stacy. "We might be lucky. He might not even be in town."

As Chad looked at her, he could read from her facial expression that even she didn't believe that.

"He's here," Chad said. "I don't know how I know, but I can feel it. He's here, and he's here to get her."

"That doesn't make sense, and you know it," Smithy said, even though she, too, was feeling doubt about everything to do with what was currently happening. "Stacy was brought here to start a new life – to keep her safe from him. Why would anyone leak to him that she was here? The only people who'd know that would be law enforcement…"

Hearing the uncertainty in her voice, Chad looked at her at the same time that she looked at him. Having known each other for as long as they had, there was no hiding the fact that neither of them knew the full story about what was happening, or why.

"Come on," Smithy finally said as she pulled up in front of the store.

Approaching the store front, at first Chad allowed himself to feel a bit more relaxed. The store was silent and there didn't appear to be anyone in it. Then he saw Ella toward the back of the store, frozen as she stared at whatever was in front of her.

Striding more quickly into the store, Chad was momentarily stunned at the sight of Stacy on the floor, unconscious.

"Don't even think about moving," he heard Smithy call out from behind him, followed by the sound of more footsteps from the doorway.

Glancing back briefly before he intended to crouch down over the woman he'd grown to have feelings for, Chad only momentarily saw the two officers run in before he felt a fist slam squarely on the side of his jaw.

"Fuck!" he called out as he tried to comprehend what had just happened.

Shaking his head to get his senses back so he could check Stacy, he caught the first glimpse of the man he'd been hoping to find.

"Get him out of here!" the voice of the sheriff called out as the two officers finally gained control of the criminal they'd been watching for a very long time.

"Stacy!" Chad called out as he leaned down. "Come on! You can't leave us yet. I only just found you!"

"Chad," Smithy said as she moved close behind him. "Chad, town medics are on their way."

"Hear that, Stacy?" Chad asked, leaning close to her as he felt tears come to his eyes. "You'll be in good hands in no time."

"I … I don't know what … what just happened?" Chad heard Ella ask, still standing in the same spot and obviously in shock.

"Everything's going to be okay now, Ella," he then heard Smithy reply. "Let's close the store for the rest of today, and I'll make you a cup of tea, huh?"

As Chad heard the voices around him, he stayed where he was. There was breath coming from Stacy. That was a good sign. Now if only she would wake up…

"Please move aside," he heard some new voices start to say minutes later.

"Chad, come away," Smithy added. "Come on, they have to do their job, to help her."

Although not wanting to leave her side, Chad did as he'd been told.

"I want to come with you," he said when he saw them carefully lift Stacy onto a stretcher and start to carry her out.

"You can follow," a stern voice said in response. It wasn't much but it was better than nothing.

Stepping out into the rain, Chad found himself in two minds. He could stay with the woman who'd recently but strongly made such a dint in his hard heart, and make sure she was okay. Or he could go with the men who'd hauled Ricky Tennyson off, and seize the opportunity to ask some much needed questions.

"He won't be going anywhere today," Smithy said as she walked up behind him. "Go and make sure Stacy's alright. The sheriff and those officers will be questioning Tennyson for hours yet, I reckon."

"They want to take him back to his hometown," Chad said, remembering some of what the sheriff had said earlier. "They already have a case against him, and that's all happening away from here. They could put him on a plane now…"

"That isn't going to happen," said Smithy. "Don't worry about that. I'm not going to let it happen."

"No offence, but you're the deputy," Chad said.

"There's one above you, and those officers are from a separate jurisdiction altogether. I don't think you'd be able to stop…"

"He just assaulted a resident of this town," said Smithy. "I won't be letting anyone take him away. Not till we can talk to him about Missy."

"You believe that he might have had something to do with that then?" Chad asked, surprised. "You believe my theory…"

"I think it's certainly worth questioning him about since he's already here and we do know he was here that day," Smithy replied without commitment. "Now go to Stacy and let me know how things are looking a little later."

Before he could object to anything, Chad saw Smithy jump in her car and drive off in the direction of the sheriff station.

"Is she alright?" he heard Ella's voice ask from behind him.

"I thought that deputy was going to make you a cup of tea," Chad said, trying to appear far more relaxed than he felt. He wanted to go to Stacy, but as his senses cleared, he knew it was always best to leave medical professionals to do their job, at least for the first short while after they began helping someone. "Come inside. I'll make you one."

"But Stacy…" Ella said, her voice betraying just how much of a shock she'd received.

"Is in good hands," Chad said even though his heart yearned to go to the woman he deeply cared for. "Right now, it's you that needs some support."

"She's a good girl," said Ella. "She never told me what happened to her but I could tell it was serious. Do you think that … that was him … the one who did … the one who treated her…"

Before Chad heard any more words from the older

woman, he saw her break down into tears, finally letting go of whatever level of stress had built in her from what she'd seen.

"She's going to be okay," Chad reassured her as he felt tears come to his eyes. He, too, wanted to go and check Stacy was going to be okay, but he couldn't leave the older woman in the state she was in. "Do you have someone who can come and be…" he started to ask before a young man came running into the store.

"Ma?!"

"Zach?" Ella asked as she pulled away from the embrace she'd allowed Chad to extend to her. "What are you doing here?"

"Smithy called me," the young man said. "You…"

"Oh, I'm alright," Ella said even though it was evident she was anything but.

"No arguing, Ma," said Zach. "You've had a shock and the shop can stay shut for the rest of the day. Come on. I'm taking you back to our place."

"There's no need to fuss…"

"Yes, there absolutely is every need to fuss, so stop being a rebel and come with me," Chad watched the young man say. "Who are you?"

"This is … oh, what is your name?" Ella asked.

"Chad. I'm an investigator…"

"Right," said Zach, as if he really didn't care. "Okay, Ma, I'm putting the closed sign on the door, and we're leaving. Come on! I can't stay away from work for long but Suzanne is at home and we're both really worried about you. Now, let's go."

Without any further argument, Chad watched the older woman let her son lead her out the door and toward his car.

"Please check on her," he saw Ella call out before she and her son drove off.

Not knowing where Stacy would have even been

taken to, Chad felt useless. Going to check on her was now out of the question since he hadn't followed the medics when they'd taken Stacy away, so had no idea where they'd gone.

Resolved that there was nothing he could do in that moment for the woman he was growing to love, he forced his mind to refocus on the cold case he'd been working. Going to see Ricky Tennyson wouldn't be easy, especially given the anger Chad felt inside for the man having done what he'd just done, but it might be Chad's one and only opportunity to get answers to the many questions he had.

Left with little choice about what to do next, he finally moved. His heart and his mind both argued that there was someone more important needing his attention, but he fought those thoughts. Stacy was in good hands. She would be in good hands long enough for Chad to get the answers he needed.

CHAPTER 40

Later, as Stacy moved in an out of consciousness, snippets of memory presented themselves to her before she would lose them again.

"Hello," she eventually heard a woman's voice say. It wasn't a voice Stacy had ever heard before. "Welcome back."

"Where … am … I?" Stacy managed to push out, determined to try and stay awake instead of falling into a slumber yet again. "What is this place?"

"Don't worry," the woman said. "You're at the hospital. You've got some injuries, but you're already on the mend."

"Hospital?" asked Stacy, confused. "I didn't know Skagway had a…"

"You're in Juneau," said the woman. "You were airlifted here earlier today."

For a long while, Stacy found she couldn't make any sense of what she was being told. Then her mind cleared and it all made sense after all.

"Juneau?!" she said, only one consideration coming to mind. "My daughter … I can't be in Juneau! I have to go back…"

Before she could get out of the bed, she felt an intense pain shoot through her entire torso, forcing her to stop.

"You shouldn't move, Ms McNab," the woman said. "You're on the mend, but you still are in quite a state."

"My daughter…" Stacy said as tears came to her eyes. "He's in town. He'll take her. He could *kill* her if it means hurting me."

"Do you mean … this little lady?" the woman asked before another walked in with Patti in her arms.

"Mommy!"

"Now, remember what we talked about, little lady?" one of the ladies said, resisting Patti's attempts to break free of her arms. "Mommy is very, very sore, and can't have very tight hugs for a few days."

"I remember," Patti said meekly.

"I'm going to sit you on the side of her bed here, but...?"

"No tight hugs," said Patti.

As Stacy listened to the conversation, she smiled through the intense tears that naturally broke forth. She was in another city, but her daughter was with her.

"There's a police guard at the door," she then heard the woman whisper in her ear. "We can send them away if you..."

"No!" Stacy said. She had no idea what the guard was there for, but if someone felt it was warranted, that was good enough reason for her. "No, that is fine, thank you."

Keeping an eye on the guard, she turned to Patti and gently pulled her as far into a hug as she could before feeling the pain increase. She had no idea what exactly had happened back in Skagway, but she was certain that Ricky had found her, and had seen her, and had done to her all that she could currently feel. Had anything been done to him because of it? Had they even caught him?

While holding Patti and reassuring her that all was okay, Stacy fought the many memories that wanted to break forth – past memories of having been beaten just as badly, and worse, and her being too afraid to try and leave. Why had she waited so long? Why hadn't she gone to the police earlier and put some trust in them helping her to be safe?

But the police had been the people who'd moved her to Skagway. How had Ricky found her? Nobody else knew where she was...

Before the thought took hold, Stacy looked at her

little Patti's face. As always it was happy and smiling.

"Did you go on a plane?" Stacy asked. The response she received – the ongoing smile that accompanied a lengthy three-year-old description of all that Patti had been through – was enough to put Stacy's fears to rest … at least for the moment.

CHAPTER 41

As Chad stood outside of the sheriff's one and only interrogation room, looking in through the glass, he found it difficult to stop his leg from pulsating. Sometimes that was the way when he found himself itching to get in front of a criminal to ask questions.

"The sheriff has got this," Smithy said as she came and stood beside Chad.

"I don't know why," Chad replied. "I've been working on Missy's case. Why is the sheriff asking the questions?"

"It's just what's happening, that's all," he saw Smithy say as she shrugged her shoulders. "Your turn will come, I'm sure."

"Yeah," said Chad, feeling surprisingly dissatisfied. It wasn't a natural way for him to feel, but he couldn't stop, especially knowing that Stacy wasn't out of the woods yet. "She woke up."

"Yeah, I heard," said Smithy, grinning. "Perhaps a trip to Juneau is on the cards for you?"

Despite the seriousness of what was going on around him, Chad delivered her the smile he knew she'd expect.

"Just knowing she's gonna be okay, and she's safe from that bastard, is enough for me," he said.

"Really?" asked Smithy. "You don't … I dunno … *miss* her … or anything?"

As always when Smithy made suggestive remarks to him, Chad chuckled.

"I do miss her," he quietly admitted, as much to himself as to Smithy. "But I do also really need to focus on this. If Tennyson has something to do with Missy's disappearance, this might be our only chance to find out where she is."

"I know," said Smithy. "At least for now he's being charged with assault. I know it's nothing compared to what he's supposed to have done…"

"And what exactly *is* that?" Chad asked, feeling his frustration begin all over again. "I still have no idea…"

"Well, what you do know is that if you have no idea about something, someone well above your pay grade has determined that you don't need to," said Smithy.

"And *your* pay grade?" asked Chad. "Is that information above that?"

"Actually, it is, so stop harassing me for information about that creep because, honestly, I don't know any more than you do," Smithy reassured him. "*Honestly*!"

"Okay," Chad replied, resigned that there was obviously much more to know about everything, but for some reason, somebody didn't want him to have access to anything more.

"Sure you don't want to head off to Juneau?"

"No, I want to tie things up here," said Chad.

"Don't let her slip away…" said Smithy.

"You know what, Deputy?" Chad asked, grinning at her. "That might just be the first and only piece of good advice you've ever given me."

"Ha!" Smithy exclaimed, laughing. "Seriously though, when did you last…"

"No more questioning, Deputy!" Chad said, cutting short a question she'd put to him more times than he could count. "Now, aren't you supposed to be going to do some work or something?"

"Looks like I … and you … are about to," said Smithy. "Ready?"

Not sure what she was talking about, Chad followed the line of sight she showed with a nod of her head. In the interrogation room, he could see the sheriff standing and looking knowingly at the glass that separated him from where Smithy and Chad stood.

"Now please, Chad, we are going in there to ask him questions about *Missy*," Smithy said, her face revealing a rare expression of utter seriousness to him. "This isn't the time to let any emotion about Stacy interfere with that."

"Got it," Chad said. He knew full well that he would love to get in that room and pummel the jerk in much the same way he'd pummeled Stacy. Chad also knew that he'd told Missy's family he was going to be re-investigating her disappearance, and he had to follow through and do the very best he could do in just that. It wasn't ideal with how he felt about Stacy, but it was just what had to be done.

CHAPTER 42

"I already answered all your questions," Ricky Tennyson said with a vicious look and tone as he addressed Chad and Smithy sitting down in front of him. "I got nothing more to say."

Clenching his fist tightly closed, Chad fought to maintain calm. It wasn't easy to push aside the state he'd seen Stacy in after the monster in front of him had done what he'd done.

"Tell us about your last time in Skagway, Mr Tennyson," Smithy began.

"The … last time?" Ricky asked. "I don't understand."

"The last time you came here," Chad said. "You came here in…"

"A couple of years ago," said Ricky. "Yeah, I was on a cruise with my wife…"

"The one you just beat up," said Chad before feeling Smithy's leg press against his own, in a clear warning sign to stay on topic.

"She took my kid!" Ricky exclaimed, as if that justified the way he'd reacted to seeing Stacy. "She had no right to do that!"

"Mr Tennyson, please do as we've asked," said Smithy. "The last time you visited Skagway - tell us about that day."

"Nothing to tell," Ricky said. "Ship pulled in, just like today. We got off, just like today…"

"And you beat a woman up, just like today?"

"What?" Ricky asked. "What the *fuck* are you talking about?"

"A young woman went missing on that day, from this town," Smithy said. "We understand that you like young woman. You like to…"

"Hey, I never done anything to anyone when I was last in this town!"

"You sure about that?" Chad asked. "You didn't run into a young woman who … I dunno … met your … *requirements…*"

Before he finished the question, he saw the suspect lean forward and speak passionately.

"Look, you wanna know what I did that day? That day – that last stinking day in this stinking town? I did what any good husband does on a cruise. I let my wife choose the excursions that she wanted to do, and I went along with her on them."

"And then?"

"And then … what?" Ricky asked. "We went and did some double-up excursion thing, on that stupid train thing first and then to some salmon bake."

"And?" Smithy nudged.

"And nothing else!" said Ricky. "That was the worst day of that fucking cruise! From the moment we docked, we had to get on a bus and a train and then another bus, and a tiny plane. It didn't end from the moment we got off the ship, until we got back on just before the ship left. Almost didn't make it, with too much on that day. I tried to tell her but she wouldn't fucking listen – *never* fucking listens!"

"And there will be a record of this somewhere?" Smithy asked. "Your excursions?"

"I … I assume so," Ricky replied. "If you know I was on that cruise on whatever day it was that whoever disappeared, then I'm guessing you *know* what excursions I did with that whore…"

Feeling his blood instantly begin to boil, Chad was saved from his immediate impulse to reach across the table, by Smithy's foot firmly moving onto his. Oh how well she knew him…

"And if that isn't enough, then there's probably still

rubbish from that day back at the house," Ricky added. "Never throw anything out, I always say. You just never know when you might have to *prove* an *alibi*."

"Do you recognize this young woman?" Chad asked, using all of his internal strength to not show just how angry and rattled he was.

"*No*, I don't recognize this woman!" Ricky replied. "Look, I admit to beating up my wife but you ain't putting whatever this is, on me! Yes, I came to Skagway on a cruise, and yes, I was with that no-fucking-good wife of mine, but we were on excursions from the moment we could get off that fucking ship, until just before it left port. Ask the company! Ask … *my wife*."

"Yeah, it's pretty convenient that she isn't saying much right now, huh," said Smithy. The grin she received from the criminal facing her almost made her vomit.

Without much more to say or to ask, Smithy made the call for her and Chad to get out of there.

"What a piece of…" Chad started to say as they walked out.

"Yep, no doubting it but…" Smithy said.

"But what?" Chad asked, in his heart already beginning to possibly question the same thing she was.

"Look, I don't know this guy – I've never met him before so don't know what his mannerisms are usually like – but I'm not sure if he does have anything to do with Missy's disappearance, Chad," said Smithy.

"He obviously has the ability to pull wool over people's eyes…"

"Yeah, that's very true, but tell me this – in all those boxes, did you see anything about the excursions he talked about?" Smithy asked.

"No," Chad replied. "I've been through those boxes more than once. There was nothing at all about the excursions he said he and Stacy went on…"

"What about excursions *other* people went on?" Smithy asked. "Were there details of those?"

"No," Chad said, shaking his head. "I'm guessing that nobody can have requested them…"

"Best you get on with that then," said Smithy. "I know you're angry about what he did to Stacy this morning, but you've got to separate yourself from that and find out what's the truth for *Missy*."

As he watched Smithy jump in her car, Chad knew she was right. There was cloudiness in his thoughts about the fact that Tennyson was Stacy's husband. He needed to work hard to keep that completely separate in what he had to find out.

"And after you do that – jump on a plane to Juneau!"

Despite all the seriousness layered upon layers inside of him, Chad grinned at Smithy before she drove away. She was a good deputy. He'd seen her move from job to job, moving up ranks sometimes and moving sideways other times, but he sincerely hoped she would eventually get the job she ultimately wanted.

"Chad," he heard a male voice call out to him from inside the small building.

Turning around he saw Sheriff Reed beckoning him to follow. Once in the sheriff's office, alongside the two officers and with the door closed, the sheriff indicated for him to sit.

"We'll be moving him," Chad heard one of the officers say. "We're taking him with us tonight…"

"What?" Chad asked, surprised. "But what about Missy…"

"Chad, you got him," the sheriff said. "We all know he did it – you know it, I know it, and these guys know it. He has a thing for young girls, and he was here that day. Pretty open and shut case, that one, don't you think?"

"No!" Chad exclaimed. "No, I *don't* think! I am

here, in your town, to find out what happened to a young woman…”

“Yes, and now we know,” the sheriff said. “Look, from what these guys have said, Tennyson is an absolute *monster*!”

“And I believe it, but I have to be sure…”

“Be sure, and let it go,” said the sheriff. “Over to you guys.”

Chad sat in disbelief as he heard one officer and then the other offer details of the plan to get Ricky Tennyson out of Skagway and back to his home town, where he would be put in jail to await what was expected to be a lengthy trial for horrific things he’d done to multiple young women.

As much as Chad wanted to object and argue that it wasn’t right, he sat quietly and pretended to accept it. He didn’t accept it at all, but he could pretend. If nothing else, at least Tennyson was going to be behind bars, even if it wasn’t because of what he appeared to have done to Missy Jameson.

“I hear you might have a … personal … reason to want to go to Juneau right now,” the sheriff said, further surprising Chad. “These guys have all of this under control so why don’t you go with them.”

“We do have to stop at Juneau on the way,” one of the officers said to him. “You can join us that far and we’ll leave you there.”

“Right,” said Chad. “I’ll … when are you leaving?”

“More of our men are on their way here now, to help with escorting Tennyson,” one officer said. “They’re due here at two, and we’ll all be on the flight out of here at four.”

“All … as in Tennyson as well?” Chad asked.

“Yep.”

“Okay,” Chad said. Whatever was going on, it all seemed to be out of his hands. “I’ll just grab some stuff.”

"We can pack up everything in your office for you…"

"Thanks but no. I'll head to Juneau and then come back to sort out everything," Chad said. "If you can just leave my office as it is…"

"Sure," the sheriff said.

With nobody having anything more to say to him, Chad left the office, grabbed a few things he wanted from it, and then headed home to pack an overnight bag. Smithy and the sheriff were right – they'd gotten the man who'd done something to Missy, and eventually that man would tell what exactly happened to her, so her family could have closure.

In the perfect world, that was exactly how things could go.

In the real world, would they?

CHAPTER 43

"Hey you," Stacy heard Chad's voice say from outside of her weary dizziness.

"Chad!" she then heard a very familiar little voice say, filled with joy, as always.

"Hey, Kiddo, how are you going?" Chad asked the little person he couldn't deny he'd taken quite a liking to.

"Good," Patti's voice said quietly.

As Stacy opened her eyes and saw Chad standing over her hospital bed with Patti in his arms, she was surprised but pleased.

"What … what are you doing here?" she asked, trying to sit up. "I thought I was in Juneau."

Hearing her sleepy confusion, Chad grinned at her before placing Patti on the bed and then leaning down to kiss Stacy softly.

"You *are* in Juneau," he said, pulling back as he gently sat on the edge of the bed. "Seems your body needed a little bit more care than what could be provided in Skagway, so I just thought I'd pop in and see how you're doing."

"I'd like to be able to say I've felt better and I've never felt anything like this before," Stacy said. "Unfortunately…"

Not hearing her finish her sentence, Chad nodded but didn't ask any questions about whatever she was going to say.

"The medical staff reckon you're going to be okay in a week or two…"

"A week or two?" Stacy asked. It was news to her. "No – Patti…"

"Is right here with you," said Chad as he affectionately messed up Patti's hair. "I can't stay long for this visit but I will definitely be back as often as I can.”

“You’re going back to Skagway already?” asked Stacy. “You only just got here.”

“I know,” Chad said, regretful that he had things to do, and things to work out. “I wish I could say that this is only a social visit, but…”

“But what?” Stacy asked, curious.

“Stacy, do you remember a cruise you went on a while back?” Chad asked.

“Yeah, of course,” Stacy replied. “That was when I saw Skagway before. It was an Alaskan cruise. Why’s that?”

“Can you remember what you did that day?” asked Chad. “Was that the first time you went up to the waterfall?”

“No,” said Stacy. “No, I didn’t see much of the town at all that day. The first time I saw the waterfall was when Smithy took me up there – just a few days before I saw you there that first time.”

“Right,” Chad said. In his heart, he didn’t want to push her for information relating to his case, and it felt wrong to do so, but he needed better closure to give Missy’s family.

“That doesn’t answer your real question,” Stacy said as she watched his face. “Maybe it would be best if you just ask your question straight out.”

Inside of her, she had a feeling of regret growing. Early on in her move to Skagway, she’d had suspicion everyone was being nice to her only because they’d eventually need something from her with regard to Ricky and whatever he’d done. To think that Chad – a man she had actually started to develop feelings for – was now proving those suspicions right, and she’d started to give her heart to a man who’d strung her along while having an ulterior motive, was enough to want her to turn over and weep. Knowing her daughter was close by, sitting on the end of her bed, she fought to make sure she wouldn't let that happen.

"What *do* you remember doing that day?" Chad asked. Over their time together, he'd seen her emotions change as certain kinds of thoughts had passed through her mind. He thought he'd gotten to know her very well in that respect, and that made her current facial expression painfully hard to see.

"We did a couple of things," Stacy said as she fought to hold back tears. She was angry at herself for having started to believe a man could actually have real feelings for her, and not want to just use her for his own gain. Even so, if he was asking questions around the time that Ricky had arrived in Skagway, Stacy knew it must be for a very good reason. If her answering questions would help some other family gain some peace, she had to push her personal feelings aside and do what she could to help. "Umm, we definitely went on that steam train trip, and then, I can't remember where we went but we flew on a small plane to some place a bit more remote, to … have salmon? Something like that. Sorry, I don't remember where it was exactly, but it wasn't in Skagway itself. If it helps, I think we kept everything from that trip – the pamphlets and stuff. It should be in the house…"

"Right," said Chad. "Do you remember if you had *any* time in the township?"

"No, none," said Stacy. "If I remember right, we only just made it back to the ship. Ricky was so angry … yeah, that should have been a sign to me back then, I suppose, but can't go back in time and change that now, right?"

Chad took some time to think about her answers. Was she telling the truth, or had Ricky Tennyson done such a good job in brainwashing her over the years that she either naturally covered for him now, or she honestly thought she'd done something he'd only drummed into her she had?

"Chad, what's all this about?" Stacy dared to ask. She suspected he wouldn't be able to tell her, and a moment later, her suspicions were proved right.

"I can't … sorry, Stacy, I can't talk about this with you," Chad said with regret. "Not now anyway."

"Okay," Stacy said, trying to deliver a sad smile even though inside her heart was truly breaking. It had seemed like a potential change in her life, getting to know a man who was kind and not going to hurt her. How stupid she'd been to think things could go that way.

Feeling the threatening tears finally succeed in pushing through, she turned away from the man she wished she'd never allowed herself to trust. Of course he was using her. Of course he needed something from her. And of course, no matter what it was that he needed from her, she would be discarded once that was done with.

"Stacy, I just can't…" Chad said as he watched her body betray her by giving clear signs she was crying, no matter how hard she was trying to hide it.

"I know," said Stacy. "I hope that whatever you've learned from my answers, does help you in your case."

With the deepest regret he'd felt in a long time, Chad leaned over and kissed her cheek as best he could from the angle he was on, gave Patti a hug, and then walked out.

Once through the swing doors at the end of the corridor, he, too, allowed himself to let out the tears that came from the knowledge and realization that he had very much fallen in love with the woman lying in that hospital bed…

And now he'd caused her hurt.

"I was wondering if I'd see you today," Chad heard the chief of police say when he wandered into his office of the police station. It should have been tiring, doing the amount of flying he'd done recently. Instead, Chad felt revved up – a feeling that came from the combination of wondering if he would finally be able to tell Missy's family what had happened to her, and the regret that came from having seen Stacy in hospital.

Throughout his final flight he'd played that conversation over and over in his mind. He hadn't meant to upset her in any way by asking the questions he had, but he'd suspected he might do so when he'd considered doing it. Hurting her in any way was the last thing he'd wanted to do, and he would never have even given the plan to ask her questions any kind of attention if he didn't desperately want to find the ultimate answer – what happened to Missy Jameson?

"I'm glad that you know me so well," Chad said as he closed the office door and sat down opposite the chief. "And that since you *do* know me so well, it won't come as any surprise why I'm here."

As he watched, he saw the chief of police relax back in his seat and quietly study Chad, as if looking for something specific. Even though Chad regarded himself as a fairly patient guy, he couldn't sit for too long before having to be proactive in finding out what he needed to know.

"I need to get into Ricky Tennyson's house," he said, knowing full well that life was never as simple as asking for something and automatically getting it.

"And what, may I ask, would you need to do that for exactly?" the chief asked, his tone telling just how many times he'd heard such a request over his long career.

"He's a suspect in the cold case I'm working," said Chad and saw the chief nod in response. "In questioning him, he reckons that even though he was in Skagway on the day that Missy Jameson went missing, he was on tours all day long and there's no way he could have done anything…"

"You know they all say things like that, Chad," the police chief said, finally leaning forward in a show of being slightly interested. "You now know who his wife is."

Hearing the chief mention that felt like a slap across Chad's face. He knew he had to keep Stacy in the forefront of his mind now that her husband was a suspect. It didn't make it any easier to be forced to confront just how deeply he felt for the woman he'd so recently met.

"I do," Chad said.

"And?" the chief asked. "I assume you've spoken to her."

"You know he just went into Skagway – as you knew he was going to – and tried to beat the living crap out of her…" said Chad, wondering how much detail had gotten back to the man in front of him.

"I have been told that, yes," said the chief. "Even so…"

"On the way here I called into the hospital in Juneau and asked her about their day in Skagway back then," Chad said.

"And?"

"And she's adamant they were doing things all day too," Chad replied. "She was pretty resolute in her insistence that they'd spent the entire day on tours, and backed up Tennyson's story that they only just made it back to the ship before it set sail."

"And you believe her?" the chief asked. "She's been controlled by this guy for a long time, Chad. You know as well as I do that sometimes these assholes reach a point where they can almost brainwash their partners."

"I know," said Chad. "And that is why I want to see if there's anything in the house to corroborate the story that both of them are saying."

"What about the cruise line itself? Surely they have records," the chief suggested.

"Yeah, of course, and the request has been put in, but it could take weeks – too long!"

Once again the two men indulged in a lengthy game of staring at each other, deep in thought, without saying anything.

"Look, I get what you're asking but there's no way I'm going to be able to get a warrant for that…"

"Don't you already have one?" Chad asked in disbelief. "I don't know the details of the case you're building against him…"

"No, you don't," the chief replied bluntly.

"But I'm assuming you already got into his house somehow," said Chad, beginning to wonder if anybody else was actually interested in figuring out what had happened to Missy. "Come on, Chief. Stacy said they kept documents from the cruise, and any details of tours they did should be among those."

"Chad, is this what's driving this request? This … somewhat *personal* interest you have in this woman? Because she is the *wife* of this guy…"

"I know that! *Now!*" Chad said. "Unfortunately nobody told me that on the day that I escorted her and Patti up there." Remembering back to that first day that he'd met her, he found himself desperately wishing he could have met her under different circumstances – *any* different circumstances. "This has nothing to do with how I feel about her…"

"You sure?" the chief asked.

"Yes!" said Chad. "I want to find out what

happened to Missy Jameson and, somehow, Ricky Tennyson seems to be tied up in that. I'm not asking for much, Chief – just to be able to see if there are any documents relating to this one day, in this one town. I'm happy to go with as many of your officers as you need to send with me to make sure I don't see or do anything else in that house."

After a long pause, Chad was pleased to see the chief nod.

"We have a warrant and we've already been through the house, but I'll approve you going in with one of my men – *only* to look for what you're talking about – documents that prove he couldn't have had time to hurt that girl," the chief said before picking up his desk phone and asking someone to come into the office. "But listen to me, Chad – what you're doing by getting involved with this girl, is not a good idea!"

"Then you should have considered that when you not only got me to escort her up there, but to even *send* her up there … I mean, *why* even do that when you knew her husband was planning a trip there? I … honestly, Chief, none of it makes any sense to me."

Seeing the chief look thoughtful, Chad suspected no more answers would be given to any question he could come up with. When an officer walked in, Chad knew he was dismissed.

Just before he and the officer walked out, he heard the chief call out to him.

"There's more going on here than you think, Chad," he said. "When you go into that house, search only for what you're after, and don't touch anything else."

Before Chad could question what he meant, he was led away.

CHAPTER 45

Lying in her hospital bed, Stacy smiled at her daughter. As always, little Patti was grinning and giggling at nothing in particular. It was always her way, and Stacy loved that. Perhaps some things that she might have seen might haunt her in some way in the future, but for now she seemed to be progressing as any toddler should. That was a relief.

Thinking back to when Stacy had seen Chad enter her hospital room and sit on the edge of her bed, she felt a new kind of sadness flow over her. She hadn't even wanted to embark on another relationship, and especially so soon after getting away from Ricky, but Chad had eased into her life slowly, getting her to trust him. Now what was to happen? Whatever they had shared, maybe none of it was real. Maybe it was all just about Ricky and whatever he'd done. Now that law enforcement had him in custody, maybe they didn't need her, and if law enforcement didn't need her, would Chad?

"Patti Cakes, Patti Cakes," she heard her daughter say as she edged a little closer on the bed.

"Hug?" Stacy asked as she held out her arms. It was a slow process, sharing affection for the moment while every part of her body ached, but hugs were something so easy to give, and meant so much.

With effort, she pushed memories of Chad aside. He had come into her life at a time when she needed to start rebuilding her confidence. If he no longer had any use for her, and she didn't see him again, well, at least she got to experience, for the first time in a very long time, what it felt like to receive affection from a man. Affection and kindness.

CHAPTER 46

Despite his apprehension about all that surrounded him in the current moment – the cold case; the way things were going with the suspect; and the way things had been left between him and Stacy – Chad fought to maintain focus on what he had to find out.

Ricky Tennyson had been adamant he had nothing to do with Missy Jameson's disappearance, even though he did have some weird attraction to hurting young women, and had been in Skagway that day. His statement alone wouldn't have made Chad question anything, especially since Tennyson had lied about multiple things law enforcement had now built a pretty solid case against him for.

No, it was Stacy's recollection that bothered him more. Was she telling the truth or did she still harbor some kind of commitment and obligation to Tennyson, with full intention of protecting him despite how he'd treated her? As odd as that sounded, Chad knew full well from a decent career in law enforcement that many women stood by their abusers rather than have them go to prison – *far* too many. Could Stacy be one of those?

In the back of his mind, he felt regret that the two of them hadn't shared more with each other than they had. It was through no bad intention that that was the case. He couldn't talk about his work, and she didn't seem to want to talk about anything that had happened to her. It was a shame that their combined issues in life had to be a wall that could remain standing between them, but it was what it was.

"She said it was in here," he said as he and an allocated officer entered the home.

Making his way to what appeared to be the living room, and opening the doors of a large sideboard, Chad then took his time to carefully take everything out and inspect it before moving onto the next thing. It took little time for him to find a photo album with enough writing over the cover to promise it would be full of whatever Stacy and Ricky had recorded on their Alaskan cruise.

Flipping through the pages, seeing photos of Stacy with a smile plastered on her face as she stood next to the man who had just beaten her so badly, Chad felt his emotions pushing to take over. He fought to hold them back. Still, seeing how happy she'd once been – or at least seemed – did leave him curious about why, how and when things had changed so much for her.

"Anything there?" he heard the officer ask him, prompting him to stop looking at the photo he had been – a photo where Stacy was smiling so much that the smile in the photo almost took Chad's breath away.

Turning one more page, he found what he was looking for. There, carefully stuck between photos obviously taken in the Skagway area, were two pamphlets – one for each tour. Merged in and around them were four tickets that clearly stated the name, day and time of each tour, and the names: Ricky Tennyson and Monica Tennyson.

Monica. Hmm. Was that the first time he'd heard her called that? It played with his head that her name wasn't Stacy McNab, as he'd known her all this time. In fact, she wasn't Stacy at all.

"Is that it?" the officer standing over him asked.

"Yep," Chad replied. "Tickets clearly saying they were on these two tours."

"Well, it says they were *booked* on those tours," said the officer as Chad took photos of the tickets and assessed whether he should take the album or not. "Is there any indication on the ticket itself that they were *on* the tours?"

Glancing at the tickets, Chad knew he had decisions

to make. The question presented to him had been a good one. Had Ricky and Stacy – Monica – actually been on the tours, or just booked them and got the tickets issued, but not gone?

"The train tickets have a train conductor click hole in them," Chad said quietly as he refused to not believe Stacy in her memory of that day. No matter what, she'd seemed to be speaking with honesty about what she remembered them doing.

Resolved that he believed he'd found something that might have influence in solving his cold case, he did what he had to do and got out of there with the officer to return to the police station.

CHAPTER 47

"You're recovering faster than we thought you would," Stacy heard a doctor say that evening. "We'll see how you go through tonight, but if there are no new issues, we think you'll be good to get home tomorrow afternoon."

"Thank you," said Stacy, relieved. As much as she appreciated all that had been done for her, she could appreciate even more just how much her new small home in her new small town had become important to her.

"You'll still have to take it easy for a while as your body fully recovers, but you should be okay doing the most basic chores at home."

Stacy nodded and watched as the doctor walked out. She wasn't even sure why she was in the hospital. Sure, Ricky had done a good number on her, but had she really needed to be moved to another town?

"Sleep now, Patti," she said as she glanced over at her daughter in a tiny cot bed nearby. It was a relief that Patti had been brought with her, and that she could stay in Stacy's hospital room, but they both needed to be in their own little home.

Turning over and reaching to turn the light off, she was reminded of the pain her husband had inflicted on her in those few short minutes in the store. She'd suffered from his hands and feet before, but she'd never seen him as savage as he had been in that moment. What had driven him to be like that, or had he been like that all along and she'd just chosen to never acknowledge it?

Just glad that she'd been informed he was in custody with the police, and had been transported back to what had been the hometown they lived in together, Stacy held out hope that she might never see him again.

She knew that was a long shot, especially with her ongoing belief that law enforcement were going to need something from her, but, for the moment, she was safe, Patti was safe, and soon they'd been going back to their new home.

CHAPTER 48

"Tennyson'll be away for a long time by the time we finish with him," the chief of police said when Chad strolled into his office.

"You sure?" Chad asked, sitting down.

"I'm absolutely sure," the chief said as he sat back in his chair and studied Chad for a long while. "We've got solid evidence for 35 of the 44 things we've been building a case to charge him with. Why do you ask?"

Pulling out his phone, Chad sat forward to show a photo of the tour tickets to the chief.

"Because I have proof that one thing he *didn't* do, is take Missy Jameson ... or do anything else to her," Chad said. He supposed some law enforcement officers might have taken the easy way out and added such a charge to someone who'd done evil things to other young women, but Chad wasn't one of those law enforcement officers. He hoped Ricky Tennyson would be put in prison for the rest of his life, for sure, but he wasn't going to try and pin something on him that Chad was certain he *hadn't* done.

Taking his time to assess the chief's body language and facial expression, Chad suddenly grew weary. He considered he was usually pretty good at solving cold cases, but this one had led him to nothing new – nothing solid anyway – and deep in his gut, he felt a gnawing at the possibility that not only was nothing about the case as it seemed, but the people around him knew it.

"I feel like there's something else going on around Missy's disappearance ... something that nobody's telling me," he said, speaking the truth of what he felt. "Is there something I need to know, Chief?"

It took some time but eventually he saw the stance of the man in front of him change. With what appeared to be a state of resolution that there was little choice but to tell the truth, Chad finally got the answer he'd been hoping to find for a long time.

"It wasn't Tennyson, and we've known that for a couple of months," the chief said.

"But you know who…" Chad surmised.

"We have had our suspicion, but thanks to you and Smithy, we now have proof of who, and we suspect we also know where," said the chief. "Where Missy has been all this time."

Chad waited in anticipation of news that would finally enable him to complete and sign off the cold case. He had no idea where he would go to next in his job, but he was still eager to let Missy's family know what had happened to their loved one.

"Well?" Chad asked when he could hardly stand to wait any longer to be told something … anything.

"Sheriff Reed," the chief finally said.

"Sheriff…?" asked Chad, confused. "The sheriff in Skagway?" Seeing the chief nod only confused Chad further. "You must be … are you insane? He's the town's *sheriff*. How could you even think…"

"We've been watching him for quite some time, Chad," the chief said. "There's no doubt it was him."

"Then … what did that have to do with Ricky Tennyson? Why was I led along that path?" Chad asked. "Why was Stacy put there?"

"I know it's a lot…"

"A lot? Chief, nothing you're saying makes any sense to me!"

"And that was what we wanted," said the chief, just as cryptically. "We needed him to think there was going to be someone in town to pin the disappearance – the murder – on."

"Tennyson."

"Yes," the chief said. "We have proof of the two of

them – Tennyson and Reed – having, let's just say, 'the same tastes', and Reed trying to set Tennyson up. Once we figured out what was happening, we knew there was a good chance of closing the cold case if we aligned a few pieces right…"

"Stacy, you mean," Chad guessed.

"Yes, she … what can I say? She was a pawn in this too, and that is regrettable but…"

"If you believe the sheriff is the one who did something to Missy, why haven't you arrested him?"

"We have … this morning," the chief replied. "He's on his way out of Skagway now, but apparently he didn't give up too much of a fight. Said it's been on his mind for all this time."

"But … what did he do to her?" Chad asked.

"We haven't got the full story yet, but before leaving town he did offer up where she is," said the chief. After a period of witnessing the silent question on Chad's face, he continued. "Gold Rush Cemetery."

Hearing that news, Chad felt his disbelief increase to another level. He'd been up that way several times, and had considered Mr Simpson's opinion that she would be there.

"Mr Simpson," he said quietly.

"What?"

"One of the men I spoke to – Mr Simpson – said he had a feeling she was buried there," said Chad. "Said he didn't have anything to really explain why he thought that, but that he had a gut feeling … and that he'd told the sheriff but Reed instantly dismissed it, saying he wouldn't follow it up."

"You know as well as I do that we can't just follow up every 'gut feeling', Chad," said the chief. "Don't beat yourself up for not doing anything about what Mr Simpson said to you."

Chad sat quiet for quite some time as he thought

about all that he'd learned in the previous few minutes.

"Is that it then?" he asked. "The cold case is solved? Is someone going to talk to the family?"

"The deputy – Smithy, is it? – said she would go and speak to them," the chief said.

"You've spoken to her then?" asked Chad.

"Yep, she's been the one helping us with this in Skagway," said the chief. "Didn't want to believe it at first, but followed your moves and discoveries while watching every way the sheriff acted, and reacted. When he didn't know anyone was watching, ultimately he unknowingly led her to some strong evidence that linked him to Missy on the day she disappeared."

Hearing how much Smithy had played a part in some kind of top secret investigation that he wasn't to know anything about, surprised Chad. He'd thought he knew her well. Did he at all?

"I can see you're in shock," the chief said. "You're probably thinking that all that you've been doing up there was a waste of time…"

"Actually that hadn't even crossed my mind, but now that you put it like that…"

"Sorry, but we had to find a way to test if our theory was right – to see if we could somehow get a reaction from Reed that would lead us to where we needed to go," said the chief. "By absolutely ruling out other possibilities about what could have happened to Missy, you did play an important part in solving what happened to her that day … even if you can't see it right now."

Chad didn't know how he felt on hearing such news. The previous weeks that he'd spent in the small town had all been for nothing? Nothing he'd done over that time had been needed at all, to find out what happened to the young woman? The discovery didn't make him happy.

Forcing himself to focus on something positive that

had come from the time – that Missy's family would now get answers, and maybe justice for their loss – he relaxed in his thinking and in his body. No, it wasn't a waste of time, what he'd been doing. And, in addition to the case, there was also something else that had come out of it all – Stacy.

But where would she stand now, with her husband caught and behind bars, awaiting trial?

"And Ricky Tennyson? Is this case of yours going to be successful?" he asked.

"No doubt," said the chief.

"You're absolutely sure?" Chad pushed.

Seeing the chief smile at him was surprising, but helped to relax Chad even further.

"From what I've heard from the deputy up there, you have formed an attachment to the young woman we helped to move up there - Tennyson's wife," the chief said.

"I have," Chad admitted. "It wasn't professional, I know."

"Well, perhaps you'll be pleased to know that we don't think it crosses any boundaries, given that you didn't know what all of this was about, and you didn't know who she was. Plus we made sure you didn't know Tennyson was going to be cruising up there," said the chief. "She might be called upon to testify about Tennyson's movements and actions during their marriage."

"Okay," Chad said. "But for her, now, what can happen? Does she have to move back here? Will she still have any support up there?"

"She's moved on from needing us, I hear," said the chief. "It sounds, from what the deputy has told me, that the young woman has settled in there nicely, along with her daughter. It'll be up to her what she wants to do from hereon in. She just needs to let us know what she's doing and where she's going to be so we can pull her into court if need be."

"But if Tennyson walks out of here, he knows where she is…" Chad said, the thought a horrific one.

"He won't be walking out," the chief reassured him. "Honestly, he's being charged with so many offences that even if he gets the absolute best lawyer, and they can make some charges go away, they won't be able to get him out for all of the ones we have strong evidence for. He's a danger to society – especially young women – and we'll make sure he stays right where he is."

"Right," said Chad, knowing full well that criminals got out of jail all the time. He chose not to dwell on that. "So what do I have to do … for any of this?"

"For now, you can head back to Skagway and box up all of that stuff," said the chief. "We will be arranging transport for it all. If there was anything in there that could have pointed to Reed being the suspect, I'm sure he's made sure it's been destroyed, but pack it up and secure it anyway, and we'll deal with that at a later date."

"And then?" asked Chad, not sure if he was dismissed or not. "Am I needed for anything else?"

"Nope, we have it all under control," the chief said. "Honestly, Chad, I know it doesn't seem like it now but you've done a great job with all that you've done. We suspected someone you didn't, but we still needed you to investigate all other possibilities so we could be sure there was no doubt, and you did that, so thank you."

The two men sat silent for a long while, studying each other while deep in thought.

"If there's nothing else you need from me, you are dismissed," the chief said, smiling.

Although it didn't feel quite right, Chad stood, reached out to shake the chief's hand, and then walked out. Once out of the office and in the sunshine, his mind felt even more hazy than it had before. What had just happened?

Returning to the hotel he'd booked into, he indulged in a long shower and then lay down on the bed. He was free to find and begin work on another cold case if he wanted to.

The question was … *did* he want to?

CHAPTER 49

"Hey, hey, you're still alive!" Stacy heard Smithy call out as Stacy and Patti made their way slowly through the small airport terminal.

"Smithy!" Stacy called back, smiling through the dull ache that still covered her body. "What are you doing here?"

"Well, I'm here to make sure you get home safely, of course," Smithy replied. "You're still a bit wobbly on your feet so let's get you outside, into the car."

Once all three were settled, Stacy saw the deputy turn and grin at her.

"Are you gonna be okay?" Smithy asked.

It was a question Stacy had been asking herself throughout the entire journey from Juneau. She didn't know the answer, but she didn't want to share that.

"Yeah, we're going to be fine now," she said. In truth, there was still a glimmer of despair that lingered over the uncertainty about what would happen with her husband. Would Ricky be charged? And if so, was the charge going to be serious enough to mean he'd be put away for a long time, unable to hurt her again? She wanted to ask those questions. She chose to keep them quietly to herself.

"Ella sends her regards," Smithy said.

"Oh, she must be run off her feet!" Stacy said as she realized she'd not given any more thought to her work since she'd left Skagway. "I need to get back…"

"Just hold your horses there, Stacy," Smithy said as they pulled up to the small cottage. "Don't panic. Ella ended up closing the store for the week, and going to stay with Zach and Suzanne."

"Oh, no! Is she alright? It's all my fault," Stacy said.

"Hardly," said Smithy. "Now let me help you inside

and get you settled."

After Stacy carefully moved to the sofa and settled into it, and Patti started to play in the far corner of the room with the toys she'd obviously missed, Stacy watched the deputy sit down beside her.

"He's locked up tight," Smithy said in almost a whisper. "You don't need to worry about him anymore."

"Are you sure?" asked Stacy. "I know people sometimes get out, and he knows where we are now."

"Honestly, he's not getting out," Smithy reassured her.

"What … what does that mean for me and Patti?" Stacy dared to ask. So far, she'd had suspicion about why she'd been moved by law enforcement in the first place, but she'd never asked anyone about the expectations. She knew now was exactly the right time to ask. "What … what are we needed for, Smithy?"

"I'm not going to lie," Smithy said. "There is a chance – a good chance – that you might be needed to testify against him in court, but you being here in Skagway is your choice. If you want to stay and continue this new life you two have set up here, you can. If you want to go somewhere else – if you'd feel safer somewhere else – I'd completely understand, but if you want my opinion…"

"Yes?" Stacy asked.

"I'm a selfish woman, Stacy," Smithy said, grinning. "Personally, I think that I, and everyone else in this town who's gotten to know the two of you, would love for you to stay. You've started to build a good home, and you've got your job at Ella's…"

"She might not want me there after what I put her through!" Stacy said.

"Rubbish!" said Smithy. "She's taking a few days off and then she'll be back into it, selling like she always does, and I know she'll welcome you back to work there when and if you're up for it."

"I don't know what's real…" Stacy mumbled as she thought about what she was hearing. Could it be that Ella would really want her to work for her again, after experiencing what she had? Was it real that Smithy genuinely wanted Stacy and Patti to stay, even with the doubts and uncertainty Stacy had felt about everyone's motivation for befriending her?

"I'm sure everything feels odd right now, but promise me something?" Smithy asked. "Don't make any big decisions about anything until you're on your feet again. Your body needs to rest and recover, and I suspect your mind does too after what you've been through. But I can promise you this – he *is* behind bars now, and that's one less thing for you to worry about."

"Thank you," said Stacy.

"Now, I have some spare time so can go and get you some food and stuff if you like," Smithy said as she stood and blatantly started to open kitchen cupboards and the refrigerator.

"You've done enough…"

"And yet again I say – rubbish!" said Smithy, laughing softly. "Looks like you need milk, at least, and maybe a few veges. How about I go and get those for you? Maybe little Patti would like to come for a ride? Give you a little alone time?"

As much as Stacy wanted to say that she didn't need to be alone and separated from her daughter, she nodded. When Stacy had been moved to Juneau, Patti had been whisked away from what had started to become a routine for her too. Perhaps it would be good for her to get out and about in the township, to see other people, even if only at the small supermarket.

"Would you like to go shopping with Smithy, Patti Cakes?" she asked. The enthusiastic smile and nod she received solidified her decision.

"We'll be back soon," Smithy said as she held out her hand to Patti.

Once the front door was closed, Stacy closed her eyes and began to take some deep breaths. A lot had happened in recent times, and it was sometimes a lot to take in and think about. She wanted to focus only on the fact that she and Patti were safe, and Ricky couldn't hurt them again. The longer she sat on the sofa, however, the more her brain wanted to force her to think about other aspects of life.

Hearing a knock on the door, she was curious. The supermarket wasn't far away but, even knowing that, it seemed far too little time that Smithy and Patti had been away.

Slowly she made her way to the door, taking care with every step to minimize the pain she felt. On opening the door, she was cast into a new level of surprise.

"Hey," she heard Chad say when they came face to face. "You don't look so good."

"Thanks," Stacy replied, chuckling as she held the door open for him. "That's what every girl wants to hear."

Happy that she at least sounded like she had a little cheekiness in her, Chad grinned as he closed the door behind him. If she could sound a little cheeky, maybe she was on the mend.

"What's up?" Stacy asked as the two of them sat on the sofa. "I thought you must have been doing something with…"

Seeing her difficulty in saying the name of her husband, Chad grimaced. Ingrained into his memory were the photos he'd seen in that photo album – the ones where she was so happy, and smiling so much. He hoped he would one day see her just as happy.

"It's all done," Chad said. "It's a very long story, and one I won't get into today, but it's done. *I'm* done. There's no more for me to work on for that."

"I guess you'll be heading off then, moving on to somewhere else to take on another case?" Stacy asked.

Despite her ongoing uncertainty about why he'd been spending so much time with her, she still felt sadness at the thought of not seeing him anymore. No matter what his intention had been, it had been nice experiencing kindness from a man.

"I could do," said Chad, feeling his heart begin to pound in his chest. What he was about to say, he'd never said to any woman before, but it had been on his mind since he'd arrived back in town. "Thing is, working on this case I've just finished, things happened that have made me think about my career, and if I want to keep doing what I've been doing, and I was just speaking with Smithy…"

"Oh, is this her doing?" Stacy asked. "Did she just … take my daughter away as part of a plan for you and me to…"

"Well, maybe," Chad said, laughing softly. "Who can know what truly goes on in *that* mind, but I'm glad to have this moment with you."

As Stacy watched him take her hand in his, and then raise it to his lips, she was entranced. She didn't want to be – not till she understood clearly where she stood with him – but she couldn't stop the feelings she'd developed for him. It was glorious, even though it was also scary.

"Why's that?" she dared to ask. Was he about to tell her all, and break the news to her that everything they'd done together had all been part of the case he was working on, or the people charging Ricky had been working on? And if he was about to say such things, did she want to hear it?

"Well, I … have some options, it seems," Chad replied. "I … that is, Smithy … wait let me figure out how to say all this! So, while you and I were both away, something happened and, to cut a very long story very short, there's likely to be an opening here for a sheriff in the very near future."

"Oh?" Stacy asked.

"Yeah," said Chad, his heartbeat pounding so loud it seemed utterly ridiculous to him.

"You … you can't be a *sheriff*, can you?" asked Stacy, wondering where his news was actually going.

Hearing her disbelief at the possibility, Chad laughed out loud. What was it about her, anyway? He still didn't know why she affected him like she did. He just knew that she *did* affect him, and greatly so.

"Not quite," Chad said before kissing her hand again. "Look, there's no way to say any of this subtly…"

"Yeah, please don't," Stacy said, allowing herself to feel a little hope. "Chad, whatever you have to tell me, please just tell me."

"Okay," said Chad. "Thing is, I … I absolutely love spending time with you, and I want … I want to *keep* spending time with you, and Smithy told me that she's been offered a promotion to town sheriff…"

"Right," Stacy said, wondering how anything he was going to say might have anything to do with her.

"Which means she's going to need a deputy sheriff," Chad finally said.

Seeing only confusion on Stacy's face, he grinned as he summed up what he wanted to say to her.

"Smithy has said she'd support my application to become a deputy and stay here in Skagway full time, and I … I want to do that, to be closer to you," Chad said.

"But … you don't want to work cold cases anymore?" Stacy asked and saw him shake his head in reply. "You don't want to travel around anymore for your work?"

"No," Chad replied.

"You want to stay in Skagway?"

"I do. If you don't think you want me around anymore, that's … fine, but … Stacy, it's important that I tell you how I feel so you know, and there's no doubt, and … I want to be with you, not just for the duration of any case, but full time, together, here in Skagway," said Chad. "I know it's a lot but…"

Not sure how his declaration was being received, he was surprised when, without any further hesitation, Stacy moved closer and tentatively placed her lips on his. He wasn't entirely sure what it meant, with her not having used words to respond in any way, but he had no desire to move away from the way her lips were caressing and moving with his, to find out.

"I would like that too," Stacy finally said, feeling

brave as passion began to build in her. "I think ... I might be a mess for a while yet – at least until Ricky is ... until I get confirmation that he'll never be out and able to hurt me again."

"I know," said Chad. "And I won't lie to you – that could take a while. Cases often do."

"None of us know what the future holds, but I am ... yeah, I would like to see where it can go for you and me, if you're sure."

"Oh, I'm sure," Chad said, grinning. "I think about you all the time."

"And Patti?" Stacy asked. "We're a package deal, you know."

"I know," said Chad. "I ... let's see how things go, yeah?" he asked and saw her nod. "Right now I just want to ask how you feel. Shall I ... apply for the job so I can stay and work here every day?" he further asked and saw her nod again. "And you'll let me keep kissing you?"

Seeing Stacy laugh and nod, even as she grimaced in pain, he felt his heart soar to a new level. She had her times when she was happy, and funny, and she had her times when she most definitely wasn't, but seeing her laugh in that moment, Chad thought he'd never seen anyone look more beautiful.

The only thing to do then was to kiss her ... and kiss her ... and then kiss her some more.

CHAPTER 51

"Well, hello handsome!" Chad heard Ella call out as he entered the souvenir store a month later. "Woohoo! What a looker!"

Despite his embarrassment at the reaction, he couldn't help but laugh as well.

"No need for that kind of carry on," he said quietly as he looked around the store. "Is…"

"Yep, she's out the back, getting some stock," Ella replied to the unasked question. "I have to say, she's looking mighty happy these days. I hear it's because there's a new deputy in town."

As Chad laughed again, he caught sight of Stacy walking into the main area of the store. She seemed oblivious to whatever was happening.

When she turned toward Ella and saw who else was there, she also grinned with obvious surprise on her face.

"You … you got it?" she asked and saw Chad grin at her, not moving from where he stood. "You … you're Skagway's deputy sheriff?" she asked and saw him nod. "You … you're *staying*? Permanently?"

"I am," Chad said as he walked toward her. "I am going to be wearing this nice uniform every working day, and I'm not going anywhere," he added before leaning down and kissing her waiting lips. "I hope you're happy about that."

"I am," said Stacy. "Very."

There was nothing more to be said.

The End

FINDING HIMSELF AGAIN

In a small seaside area of Sydney, Australia, 28-year-old Tom Santini has recently returned to the outside world after ten long years in jail following an error of judgment in his youth. Readjustment hasn't been easy but luck has taken a turn for him. The woman that his brother, Graham, has been seeing, is a woman with connections. Through her, Tom has finally found an employer who will give an ex-criminal a chance to start over. It hasn't been an easy six months since his release, but Tom is learning to face his situation with reality and step up to take responsibility for his decisions.

Settled in his job at Toby's Stop'n'Dine, Tom's attention is captured by a young woman who enters. She's beautiful and alluring but, seeing and talking to her, he can deeply sense her being on the run from something … or someone.

Cat is smart, sexy, and a woman who will make him wonder if he does, in fact, have a chance at being happy in love, despite his past. But why does she spook so easily? What - or who - is she on the run from? Tom knows that whatever happens, he has to think before he acts. He is determined to do things differently when it comes to dealing with difficult situations. He's already missed out on so much. He can't go back to prison.

What can he do to calm and keep safe the woman he so recently met but who already has made a difference in his life? How can he save the woman with a deep-seated passion that drives him crazy…

A POWER MOORE INVESTIGATION TALE
CATCH A CATFISH KILLER
DIANE PRATLEY

CATCH A CATFISH KILLER

After a suspicious gas explosion wakes a usually
peaceful community, what is left of the home reveals
the charred remains of Bob Masters, a hospital orderly
who has a solid reputation as someone good-hearted and
caring. When fire scene investigators confirm their
findings that the explosion was intended, so begins a
murder investigation. The one question that's on
everyone's mind is why? *Why* would anyone
intentionally try to hurt such a kind
and hard working man?

Called in to work out what could have gone wrong in
what appears to be a simple, quiet life, and who could be
behind such a horrific act, Special Agents Ashley Power
and Tim Moore start to realize how much more to
someone's life there can be other than what
people see from the outside.

Embark on a murder mystery involving crime solving of
the digital kind. Initially, through studying online actions
and conversations, it becomes evident that catfishing - an
unfortunate and sad aspect of modern day dating - seems
to be at the root of what begins to be a pattern. Even
knowing this, the journey of discovery the agents
are taken on still surprises them.

Catfishing: a deceptive activity in which a person creates
a fictional persona or fake identity on a social
networking service, usually targeting a specific victim.
With it being such an easy way to take advantage of
people in the modern age, it may take quite some
detective work to solve the mystery of who is ever
behind any screen, at any time.

TIGER IN OUR HOUSE

ANN M PRATLEY

TIGER IN OUR HOUSE

When Alana Templeton goes to do the simple task of hanging her laundry outdoors, she becomes aware that something is not as it should be in her yard. The sound she hears is one that many people might not recognize at first. For Alana, it is, surprisingly, a sound she's heard before.

Being in the yard, with her toddler in the doorway of their home, she knows the right thing to do is whatever she can to save him. The previous time, she succeeded, but will she this time?

A woman and her infant being put in danger of being attacked by the large animal that has escaped the local wildlife park, not once but twice, prompts an investigation into whether there might be more than just bad luck behind the two events. It seems unlikely that someone could have used such a beast for an attempt on someone's life. Then again, it seems unlikely that the animal would escape its confine and end up at the same location two times in a row.

Sent to figure out what might be behind the strange occurrences, Special Agents Ashley Power and Tim Moore begin to delve into an elaborate and rather unconventional scheme to hurt someone through an act of revenge.

A POWER MOORE INVESTIGATION TALE
HOME BY THE SEA
ANN M PRATLEY

HOME BY THE SEA

A decade ago, homeless people began disappearing from
four neighboring towns. Day to day, the commuters
making their way to and from work never took notice of
the less fortunate they passed. They didn't notice as the
number of homeless reduced. They didn't even notice
when entire groups of homeless people vanished.

A young woman, eager to find out where her grandfather
disappeared to, began trying to find him. When
four police departments dismissed her, telling her that
her grandfather would no doubt turn up when he
wanted to, she was too young to realize she
should pursue the matter further.

Now, ten years on, she's stepped up and pushed harder
for something to be done to find not only her grandfather
but also the countless other people who seemed to have
disappeared around the same time.

Called in to investigate the disappearances, Special
Agents Ashley Power and Tim Moore find themselves
searching for - and finding - so much more than
they thought they would.

A POWER MOORE INVESTIGATION TALE
RESOLUTION
of
HAPPINESS
ANN M PRATLEY

RESOLUTION OF HAPPINESS

Fiona Thompson - better known as Flo to everyone
who knew her - took a plunge and stepped out of her
comfort zone and into the world of online dating.
With persistence she found her prince.
He ticked all the boxes.
He was handsome. He was financially secure.
He loved her. He married her.

She was warned by friends and family that there was
something off about him. She didn't listen.

Then she woke up cold, inside the darkness
of a wooden box.

Join Special Agents Ashley Power and Tim Moore as
they investigate the disappearance of Flo, going on a
surprising journey that nobody in Flo's world could
possibly anticipate.

CHISHOLM MANOR
SERIES
~Historical Romance~

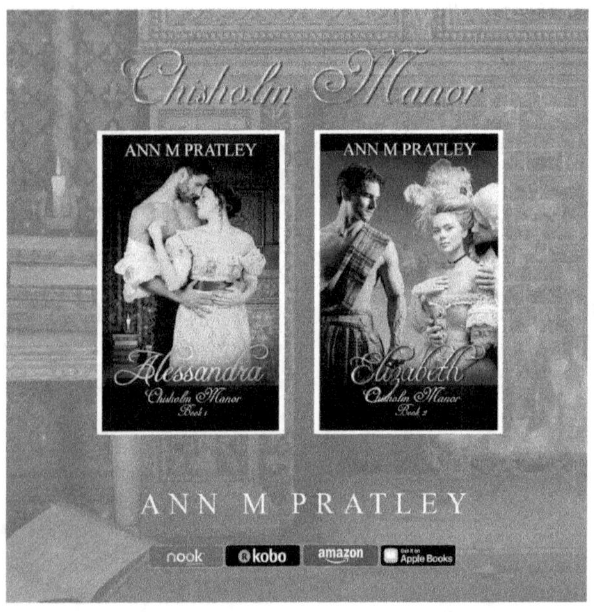

ALESSANDRA
(CHISHOLM MANOR SERIES - BOOK #1)

Passion can come from great innocence.

After receiving news from her parents of a possible betrothal, Alessandra, an 18 year old with an ingrained belief that no-one would ever wish to marry her, finds herself in a love so great that at times she cannot breathe. Married to someone as inexperienced as herself, she finds herself on a sexual journey of learning and exploration.

The combination of their mutual inexperience contributes to Alessandra discovering a degree of emotional and physical love that she has never before realized could exist.

But that love will be tested by someone from her past with sinister intentions. Jealous of the physical love Alessandra shares with her husband, he is set on doing whatever it takes to have the woman he desires, no matter the cost.

ELIZABETH
(CHISHOLM MANOR SERIES - BOOK #2)

When innocence and scoundrel collide…

When Elizabeth Chisholm visits Venice with her family, she is unexpectedly drawn to Lord Byron - a man eleven years her senior. What she sees him present to her is grace, gentlemanlike behavior, and an enthusiasm to pursue her. What she doesn't see is how much of a scoundrel he is - something he can easily hide from a mind and a heart as pure as hers.

Having grown up watching the deep and intense love of her parents - Alessandra and Edward - Elizabeth does all that is asked of her day to day but, now the age of eighteen, deeply yearns for someone to love her. The attention she receives from the handsome lord nicely fits into her desires, but where does she fit into his?

As Elizabeth is lured into the ongoing uncertainty of Lord Byron's attention, a young Scotsman wants to overcome his intense shyness. The love of art is something that he shares with Elizabeth, but he knows he can't compete with the confidence and handsomeness of the English lord.

At the request of Elizabeth's brother, Charles, the young Scotsman proves his worth by attempting to draw Elizabeth away as more things are learned about Lord Byron's actions across Europe, but is it too late? Is the reputation of Elizabeth Chisholm already sealed and irreparable, just through being associated with the scandalous English gentleman?

FORBIDDEN CONFLICTS
SERIES
~Family Saga / Romantic Suspense~

AMETHYST OF YOUTH
(FORBIDDEN CONFLICTS SERIES - BOOK #1)

The youngest member of the Stonewarden family,
Charlotte (Charlie), is 18 years old. As with everyone in
her family when they reach that age, she's been told that
when she turns 19, she'll be recruited into the family
business. She has her warning that she has one year to do
anything else she wishes to do - travel, study, work.
Whatever she wants to do, she has 365 days to
do it. On her next birthday, her life will
effectively stop being her own.

But Charlie wants nothing to do with the business.
The youngest of six, with five older brothers, she wants
a different life. Maybe if the family business was
something normal like a retail shop or a business
centered around trade, she'd feel differently. There
are people who say that her family's long term history
of robbing from the rich and providing to the poor is a
good thing. To her, all she can see is that they are
thieves. Plain and simple.

Her view is further secured when she and her older
brother, Max, are shot at in a local supermarket. Seeing
Max lying in blood and later lying unmoving in hospital
in a coma, pushes her further in her resolve to find a way
to not take part in the activities of her father and brothers.

At the shootout she is saved by a checkout operator, Ash.
Whilst building their friendship, Charlie will learn things
about her family that she didn't particularly wish to
know. She will hear more and more that she can't
share with Ash and, the more she learns,
the wider the gap will become.

In years she's young, but having lost her mother when she was only nine years old, Charlie has an older soul. The possibilities she'll be presented with during her one final year of her own will push her in her considerations of how she really wants her life to be. She wants one thing. Her strict ex-military father wants another. The dynamics of her new friendship will pull her in a third direction.

How will she choose what's right for her? And what would she have to do to break free from the chains that she can see her father wants to place around her for the rest of her life?

REVIEWERS SAY:
"This was a good clean romance with plenty of action to further the story along ... will make you ponder about life's situations, their actions and reactions, and how the decisions of past generations can affect the current ones. You'll be glad you read it!"

"... loved this book! It took me by surprise--great from start to finish! I don't normally read crime family dramas, but I love coming-of-age novels. Charlie is on the cusp of being inducted into her family's Robin Hood-esque biz, but she doesn't want that. She isn't sure what, exactly, she does want...just not THAT. Her connection with Ash furthers that disconnect, and they stumble through the beginnings of young love together. Of course, secrets and family craziness threaten their romance at every turn. ...It's an awesome start to the Forbidden Conflicts series!"

"A wonderful read. A timeless push and pull between our own wants and our family's wants. Will she follow the path her family wants or will she follow her own path? Read the book to find out."

RUBY OF LAW
(FORBIDDEN CONFLICTS SERIES - BOOK #2)

For generations the Leadbetters have lived off crime. For as long as any of them know, fathers and mothers have taught sons and daughters how to succeed in the criminal world, primarily through theft.

Phillip Leadbetter is 29 and has devoted his whole life so far to doing what his father and mother have told him to do. The sacrifice for doing that is that he still lives at home and hasn't yet met anyone who he believes could accept the man that he is because of his family.

One night a potential tragedy brings him into the path of Daisy, an up and coming professional in the legal sector. Seeing him as her knight in shining armor, she can't stop thinking about the rugged guy who saved her. She's also very pleased when fate brings their paths to cross again.

Getting to know one another, both leave out major details about who they are. She doesn't want him to know she's a lawyer because some people just don't like lawyers. He doesn't want to tell her about his family and their long history of criminal activity.

How, then, will things turn when they meet up in a courthouse, each learning in that moment who the other really is? How will they deal with the fact that she is on one side of the law, and he is very definitely on the other?

DIAMOND OF WAR
(FORBIDDEN CONFLICTS SERIES - BOOK #3)

James Stonewarden is a playboy. He has been since the moment he first started to notice girls. He loves them all, and they all love him. Why would he want to get himself into a relationship?

Sasha Leadbetter's a hot-headed young woman, known to the law for her quick temper and harsh ways. She isn't one to mess with - especially with the way she keeps a blade in her pocket. To her it's her security. It's something that makes her feel safe and comfortable. She's had it for so long that it's nothing for her to pull it out and hold it to someone's throat without any conscious thought.

Unaware of who each other are, or how their families are distantly interconnected through crime, the chance of James Stonewarden meeting Sasha Leadbetter is slim. But it happens.

A playboy and a young woman who has the mentality to kill. What kind of recipe could that result in? And what will happen when James identifies a car at Sasha's family home, that matches the description his sister Charlie gave after the supermarket shooting months earlier?

SAPPHIRE OF PREJUDICE
(FORBIDDEN CONFLICTS SERIES - BOOK #4)

Greg and Rhett. They've grown up together since they were teenagers. They've fought together. They've stolen together. They've even loved women together. But something deeper has existed in one of them for years. He's hidden it well. Being part of the great Leadbetter gang and family, the prejudice of certain situations has always been loudly expressed by many of its members - too many, and certainly enough to make anyone fearful of what would happen if feelings were revealed and brought out into the open.

A night has passed when finally, in a moment of wondering if he'd survive till morning, Rhett's taken the chance and kissed the person of his desire. Given their circumstances, what can they do, and where can they go?

Meanwhile, as Phillip Leadbetter continues on his path of happiness with his Daisy, someone from her past has grown obsessed with her and wants her back. To what degree will he put into effect a plan to get her back, and get Phillip out of her life forever?

~~ NOTE: This book does contain adult sexual content and LOTS of swear words.

EMERALD OF WISDOM
(FORBIDDEN CONFLICTS SERIES - BOOK #5)

When Mitchell Stonewarden lost his wife to cancer more than a decade ago, he vowed to never give his heart to anyone else. With all of his children now adults, and a new generation of Stonewardens having already begun, he's finally started to wonder - does he really want to be alone for the rest of his life? The handover of the family business to his oldest son, Vic, has seemed to be free of difficulty or issues - but has it? Mitchell knows little of his oldest son's private life away from the family. He is surprised by what is brought to his attention that he had no idea about.

While Mitchell finally starts to move on into a new chapter of his life, another of his sons - Max - is on his own path of discovery in life and in love. Previously well-known as 'Romeo' to his family and peers, he begins to wonder if Christie - a surprising addition to his life - has grown to become more important to him than any other young woman he's ever met. When her work at a homeless shelter tests the boundaries of her safety, Max's commitment to her is also tested, making him wonder if he will, indeed, end up hurting her.

Meanwhile, on the other side of town, the Leadbetter family is shattered by an unexpected turn of events that leaves Stacey wondering if she is going to lose the man she's loved for more than three decades...

PAINFUL DELIVERANCE
SERIES
~Erotic Romance/Romantic Suspense~

PAINFUL DELIVERANCE
(PAINFUL DELIVERANCE SERIES - BOOK #1)

She just wasn't made to inflict pain.

She knows it is nothing abnormal. She knows others enjoy it. But with every new level of pain he directs her to deliver to him, Alexis feels another piece of her soul die. He has wealth and he has power, and she knows he won't easily let her go.

But she has to leave. Escape. Move on. Forget. She has reached her limit of what she can do. The plans are in place to get away. She just has to hope that wherever she goes - whoever she meets - she won't find herself in exactly the same situation again.

REVIEWERS SAY:
"Something captivated me right off the bat...plot was intriguing and the pacing spot on, while the transitions between past (flashbacks) and present were easy to follow....I would recommend this to readers looking for a captivating plot, dynamic characters...great erotic passages."

"First, let me start off saying that this is a book that is unlike any other that I have ever read. Plainly stated, it is believable and raw in a way that is captivating ... Will I read the next one? YES!!!... I would say that you would really have to read this to understand... to get how believable it is."

"From the opening few pages, this book draws you into the story...I found the book hard to put down. The author does a great job interlacing the flashbacks with the present to form a tight story line."

DARKNESS OF HEART
(PAINFUL DELIVERANCE SERIES - BOOK #2)

She thought he'd stopped looking. He hadn't.

She got away from him to start a new life. She moved on. But in his mind, he still loves her and needs her. He still believes that she loves him. That she is meant to be his. That he is meant to be hers.

He will not give up searching for her. He will not give up *fighting* for her. He will pursue her and stop at nothing to get her back. But it will come at a cost … a sacrifice much greater than he will see coming. A sacrifice that will finally wake him up and bring him back to stark reality.

FRIENDSHIP OF DESIRE
(PAINFUL DELIVERANCE SERIES - BOOK #3)

Tom and Samantha. Feisty friends from childhood who feel like they know each other inside out, until the day comes when one of them suggests they go to a BDSM club together, and become formal play partners. Pushing the limits of what each of them can individually stand in their lifelong friendship, they attract and repel like magnets, until the time comes when they must choose how they will relate to one another - and what kind of relationship they will go on to have in the future.

Whilst on this journey of discovery, the two of them meet and make a new friend - Alexis. A young woman with a hidden and secretive past, and a mystery surrounding the relationship she has - or has had - with a renowned business entrepreneur who begins to integrate himself into Samantha's life, unknown to any of them whether he has done it for him, or for her … or for Alexis, being the mysterious link from his past.

REVIEWERS SAY:
"While this book is billed as the third in a series, I would classify it more as a spin-off … I enjoyed this book. Samantha and Tom's relationship was sweet. Their exploration and experimentation, and how it stressed the boundaries of their (frustratingly) platonic friendship was fun to read about. Fans of Ms. Pratley's first books in the Painful Deliverance series will surely enjoy this more intimate peek into Samantha and Tom's relationship."

Total Freedom
Series
~Contemporary Romance~

TOTAL FREEDOM
(TOTAL FREEDOM SERIES - BOOK #1)

For Debbie King, life began feeling like it was all too difficult - like she would never achieve, she would never have friends, and she would simply never fit in. But when she meets someone new who seems just like her, with low self-esteem and no belief in themselves and what they have to offer, Debbie finds the strength to focus more on them and less on herself.

So begins an incredible journey of friendship and love that will be tested by other people entering their world, and the shared passion they have for their musical talents and career together. It is a deep friendship that will be tested over and over again by events and an ongoing uncertainty over what their relationship should really be like.

REVIEWERS SAY:

"The overall story was great and hooked me right in. I had to stay with them for the entire journey ... you know it's a good story when you wish it didn't have to end."

"... an incredible job developing complex characters that are emotionally scarred and then allowing the reader to really understand their pain ... a terrific coming of age story surrounding a triangle of young characters, Debbie, Craig and Steven."

"Covered a lot of different things that can happen as we grow and was appealing for that reason."

TOTAL NEW BEGINNINGS
(TOTAL FREEDOM SERIES - BOOK #2)

In her early adulthood Debbie made a choice. She had
two men who loved her. She chose one.
She lost the friendship of the other.

Twenty years on, horrific tragedy strikes. Mother to
three grown children, she has to find the strength to be
there for them, while pushing her own grief aside.
Dealing with the loss of the man who has been by her
side for two decades pushes her into depression. Every
day seems harder to deal with than the last. The feeling
of loss is further heightened by finding her husband's
lifetime of journals. Hesitant at first to look inside them,
she eventually does. Almost instantly she regrets that
decision. In the years of her husband's writing she reads
things that lead her to seriously question whether
she ever really knew him at all, or if they had
actually been strangers for two decades.

The combination of the loss of her husband, and the
uncertainty about who he really was, pushes her to retire
into a dark room and have no desire to leave. She wants
to shut out the world. She wants to not believe what
she knows in her heart is reality.

With her youngest daughter, Poppy, still living at home,
Debbie is eventually pulled from the darkness by her
daughter's pleas. Finally the dark days start to fade and
Debbie can start to see the sun shining once more.
Finally she can find the strength to keep going. Finally
she can start to move into a period of recovery and
growth. Finally she can accept that it's okay to
accept help and lean on others.

As she starts rediscovering her ability to embrace life
again, results appear from her daughter's determination
to help her mother. Someone from her past is brought
back into her life. A friendship is re-established. It's
time to let go of the past and begin a new future.
It's time for total new beginnings.

Did you ever hear the words in your head … 'what if'?
What if you chose one path earlier in life but later had
the chance to walk down the path previously
unchosen? Would you?

THANK YOU!

Writing is something that I love to do, whether in romance, crime solving, paranormal, time travel, or something far more spicier, and I do appreciate the time you've invested into reading this story.

Every second month, I send out a newsletter to my subscribed readers, enabling them to learn about new releases and freebies, and take part in the odd opportunity to win items such as books, Amazon gift cards, and Kindle e-readers. If this sounds like something you might be interested in, you can sign up at **http://eepurl.com/ca559H**

~~~~~

If you would like to make contact with me, please:
Follow me on Bookbub
https://www.bookbub.com/authors/ann-m-pratley

Follow Me On X / Twitter
https://x.com/runkiwiwriter

Thank you,
Ann M Pratley
~~~~~